Goosebumps TV Special

②

Welcome to Camp Nightmare

Piano Lessons Can Be Murder

Goosebumps TV Special

2

Welcome to Camp Nightmare

Piano Lessons Can Be Murder

R.L. Stine

Hippo

Scholastic Children's Books,
Commonwealth House, 1–19 New Oxford Street, London WC1A lNU, UK
a division of Scholastic Ltd
London ~ New York ~ Toronto ~ Sydney ~ Auckland

First published in this edition by Scholastic Ltd, 1997

Welcome to Camp Nightmare
Piano Lessons Can Be Murder
First published in the USA by Scholastic Inc., 1993
First published in the UK by Scholastic Ltd, 1994
Copyright © Parachute Press, Inc., 1993

GOOSEBUMPS is a trademark of Parachute Press, Inc.

ISBN 0 590 19865 3
All rights reserved

Typeset by Contour Typesetters, Southall, London
Printed by Cox & Wyman Ltd, Reading, Berks

10 9 8 7 6 5 4 3 2 1

CONTENTS

Welcome to Camp Nightmare

I stared out of the dusty window as the camp bus bounced over the narrow, winding road. I could see sloping red hills in the distance beneath a bright yellow sky.

Stumpy white trees lined the road like fence posts. We were way out in the wilderness. We hadn't passed a house or a farm for nearly an hour.

The bus seats were made of hard blue plastic. When the bus hit a bump, we all bounced up off our seats. Everyone laughed and shouted. The driver kept growling at us, shouting at us to pipe down.

There were twenty-two kids going to camp on the bus. I was sitting in the back row on the aisle, so I could count them all.

There were eighteen boys and only four girls. I guessed that the boys were all going to Camp Nightmoon, which is where I was going. The girls were going to a girls' camp nearby.

3

The girls sat together in the front rows and talked quietly to each other. Every once in a while, they'd glance back quickly to sneak a look at the boys.

The boys were a lot louder than the girls, cracking jokes, laughing, making funny noises, shouting out stupid things. It was a long bus ride, but we were having a good time.

The boy next to me was called Mike. He had the window seat. Mike looked a bit like a bulldog. He was chubby, with a round face and pudgy arms and legs. He had short, spiky black hair, which he scratched a lot. He was wearing baggy brown shorts and a sleeveless green T-shirt.

We had been sitting together the whole trip, but Mike didn't say much. I thought he must be shy, or maybe very nervous. He told me this was his first time at a camp.

It was my first time, too. And I have to admit that, as the bus took me further and further from home, I was already starting to miss my mum and dad just a little.

I'm twelve, but I've never really stayed away from home before. Even though the long bus ride was fun, I had this sad kind of feeling. And I think Mike was feeling the same way.

He pressed his chubby face against the window and stared out at the red hills rolling past in the distance.

"Are you okay, Mike?" I asked.

4

"Yeah. Of course, Billy," he replied quickly without turning round.

I thought about my mum and dad. Back at the bus station, they had seemed so serious. I suppose they were nervous, too, about me going off to camp for the first time.

"We'll write every day," Dad said.

"Do your best," Mum said, hugging me harder than usual.

What a weird thing to say. Why didn't she say, "Have a good time"? Why did she say, "Do your best"?

As you can tell, I'm a bit of a worrier.

The only other boys I'd met so far were the two in the seat in front of us. One was called Colin. He had long brown hair down to his collar, and he wore silver sunglasses so you couldn't see his eyes. He acted pretty tough, and he wore a red bandanna on his forehead. He kept tying and untying the bandanna.

Sitting next to him in the seat on the aisle was a big, loud kid called Jay. Jay talked a lot about sports and kept bragging about what a good athlete he was. He liked showing off his big, muscular arms, especially when one of the girls turned round to check us out.

Jay teased Colin a lot and kept wrestling with him, gripping his head in a headlock and messing up his bandanna. You know. Just kidding around.

5

Jay had wild, bushy red hair that looked as if it had never been brushed. He had big blue eyes. He never stopped grinning and horsing around. He spent the whole trip telling terrible jokes and shouting things at the girls.

"Hey—what's your name?" Jay called to a blonde-haired girl who sat at the front by the window.

She ignored him for a long time. But the fourth time Jay called out the question, she turned round, her green eyes flashing. "Dawn," she replied. Then she pointed to the red-haired girl next to her. "And this is my friend Dori."

"Hey—that's amazing! My name is Dawn, too!" joked Jay.

A lot of the other boys laughed, but Dawn didn't crack a smile. "Nice to meet you, Dawn," she called back to him. Then she turned back to the front.

The bus bounced over a hole in the road, and we all bounced with it.

"Hey, look, Billy," Mike said suddenly, pointing out of the window.

Mike hadn't said anything for a long time. I leaned towards the window, trying to see what he was pointing at.

"I think I saw a wildcat," he said, still staring hard.

6

"Huh? Really?" I saw a clump of low, white trees and a lot of jagged, red rocks. But I couldn't see any wildcats.

"It went behind those rocks," Mike said, still pointing. Then he turned towards me. "Have you seen any towns or anything?"

I shook my head. "Just desert."

"But isn't the camp supposed to be near a town?" Mike looked worried.

"I don't think so," I told him. "My dad told me that Camp Nightmoon is past the desert, right out in the woods."

Mike thought about this for a while, frowning. "Well, what if we want to phone home or something?" he asked.

"They probably have phones at the camp," I told him.

I glanced up in time to see Jay toss something up towards the girls at the front. It looked like a green ball. It hit Dawn on the back of the head and stuck in her blonde hair.

"Hey!" Dawn cried out angrily. She pulled the sticky, green ball from her hair. "What *is* this?" She turned to glare at Jay.

Jay giggled his high-pitched giggle. "I don't know. I found it stuck under the seat!" he called to her.

Dawn scowled at him and heaved the green ball back. It missed Jay and hit the rear window, where it stuck with a loud *plop*.

7

Everyone laughed. Dawn and her friend Dori made faces at Jay.

Colin fiddled with his red bandanna. Jay slumped down low and raised his knees against the seat in front of him.

A few rows ahead of me, two grinning boys were singing a song we all knew, but with really gross words replacing the original words.

A few other kids began to sing along.

Suddenly, without warning, the bus squealed to a stop, the tyres skidding loudly over the road.

We all cried out in surprise. I bounced off my seat, and my chest hit the seat in front of me.

"Ugh!" That hurt.

As I slid back in the seat, my heart still pounding, the bus driver stood up and turned to us, leaning heavily into the aisle.

"Ohh!" Several loud gasps filled the small bus as we saw the driver's face.

His head was enormous and pink, topped with a mop of wild, bright blue hair that stood straight up. He had long, pointed ears. His huge red eyeballs bulged out of their dark sockets, bouncing in front of his snoutlike nose. Sharp white fangs drooped from his gaping mouth. A green liquid oozed over his heavy black lips.

As we goggled in silent horror, the driver lifted back his monstrous head and uttered an animal roar.

The driver roared so loudly that the bus windows rattled.

Several kids shrieked in fright.

Mike and I both ducked down low, hiding behind the seat in front of us.

"He's turned into a *monster*!" Mike whispered, his eyes wide with fear.

Then we heard laughter at the front of the bus.

I raised myself up in time to see the bus driver reach one hand up to his bright blue hair. He tugged—and his face slid right off!

"Ohhh!" Several kids shrieked in horror.

But we quickly realized that the face dangling from the driver's hand was a mask. He had been wearing a rubber monster mask.

His real face was perfectly normal, I saw with relief. He had pale skin, short, thinning black hair, and tiny blue eyes. He laughed, shaking his head, enjoying his joke.

"This fools 'em every time!" he declared, holding up the ugly mask.

A few kids laughed along with him. But most of us were too surprised and confused to think it was funny.

Suddenly, his expression changed. "Everybody out!" he ordered gruffly.

He pulled a lever and the door slid open with a *whoosh*.

"Where are we?" someone called out.

But the driver ignored the question. He tossed the mask onto the driver's seat. Then, lowering his head so he wouldn't bump the roof, he quickly made his way out of the door.

I leaned across Mike and stared out of the window, but I couldn't see much. Just mile after mile of flat, yellow ground, broken occasionally by clumps of red rock. It looked like a desert.

"Why are we getting out here?" Mike asked, turning to me. I could see he was really worried.

"Maybe this is the camp," I joked. Mike didn't think that was very funny.

We were all confused as we pushed and shoved our way off the bus. Mike and I were the last ones off since we'd been sitting at the back.

As I stepped onto the hard ground, I shielded my eyes against the bright sunlight, high in the afternoon sky. We were in a flat, open area. The bus was parked beside a concrete platform, about the size of a tennis court.

10

"It must be some kind of bus station or something," I told Mike. "You know. A drop-off point."

He had his hands shoved into the pockets of his shorts. He kicked at the ground, but didn't say anything.

On the other side of the platform, Jay was in a shoving match with a boy I hadn't met yet. Colin was leaning against the side of the bus, being cool. The four girls were standing in a circle near the front of the platform, talking quietly about something.

I watched the driver walk over to the side of the bus and pull open the luggage compartment. He began pulling out bags and suitcases and carrying them to the concrete platform.

A couple of boys had sat down on the edge of the platform to watch the driver work. On the other side of the platform, Jay and some other boys were having competitions, tossing little red pebbles as far as they could.

Mike, his hands still buried in his pockets, stepped up behind the sweating bus driver. "Hey, where are we? Why are we stopping here?" Mike asked him nervously.

The driver slid a heavy black case from the back of the luggage compartment. He completely ignored Mike's questions. Mike asked them again. And again the driver pretended Mike wasn't there.

11

Mike made his way back to where I was standing, walking slowly, dragging his shoes across the hard ground. He looked really worried.

I was confused, but I wasn't worried. I mean, the bus driver was calmly going about his business, unloading the bus. He knew what he was doing.

"Why won't he answer me? Why won't he tell us anything?" Mike demanded.

I felt bad that Mike was so nervous. But I didn't want to hear any more of his questions. He was starting to make me nervous, too.

I wandered away from him, making my way along the side of the platform to where the four girls were standing. Across the platform, Jay and his buddies were still having their stone-throwing contest.

Dawn smiled at me as I came closer. Then she glanced away quickly. She's really pretty, I thought. Her blonde hair gleamed in the bright sunlight.

"Are you from Center City?" her friend Dori asked, squinting at me, her freckled face twisted against the sun.

"No," I told her. "I'm from Midlands. It's north of Center City. Near Outreach Bay."

"I *know* where Midlands is!" Dori snapped snottily. The other three girls laughed.

I could feel myself blushing.

"What's your name?" Dawn asked, staring at me with her green eyes.

"Billy," I told her.

"My bird's name is Billy!" she exclaimed, and the girls all laughed again.

"Where are you girls going?" I asked quickly, eager to change the subject. "I mean, what camp?"

"Camp Nightmoon. There's one for boys and one for girls," Dori answered. "This is an all-Camp Nightmoon bus."

"Is your camp near ours?" I asked. I didn't even know there was a Camp Nightmoon for girls.

Dori shrugged. "We don't know," Dawn replied. "This is our first year."

"All of us," Dori added.

"Me, too," I told them. "I wonder why we've stopped here."

The girls all shrugged.

I saw that Mike was lingering behind me, looking even more scared. I turned and made my way back to him.

"Look. The driver has finished carrying out our stuff," he said, pointing.

I turned in time to see the driver slam the luggage compartment door shut.

"What's happening?" Mike cried. "Is someone picking us up here? Why did he unload all our stuff?"

"I'll go and find out," I said quietly. I started to jog over to the driver. He was standing in front of the open bus door, mopping his perspiring forehead with the short sleeve of his tan driver's uniform.

He saw me coming—and quickly climbed into the bus. He slid into the driver's seat, pulling a green sun visor down over his forehead as I walked up to the door.

"Is someone coming for us?" I called in to him.

To my surprise, he pulled the lever, and the bus door slammed shut in my face.

The engine started up with a roar and a burst of grey exhaust fumes.

"Hey—!" I screamed and pounded angrily on the glass door.

I had to leap back as the bus squealed away, its tyres spinning noisily on the hard ground. "Hey!" I shouted. "You don't have to run me over!"

I stared angrily as the bus bounced onto the road and roared away. Then I turned back to Mike. He was standing beside the four girls. They were all looking upset now.

"He—he's left," Mike stammered as I approached them. "He's just *left* us here in the middle of nowhere."

We gazed down the road at the bus until it disappeared over the darkening horizon. We all grew very quiet.

A few seconds later, we heard the frightening animal cries.

Very close. And getting closer.

"Wh-what's that?" stammered Mike.

We turned in the direction of the shrill cries.

They seemed to be coming from across the platform. At first, I thought that Jay and Colin and their friends were playing a joke on us, making the animal cries to frighten us.

But then I saw the scared, wide-eyed expressions on their faces. Jay, Colin, and the others had frozen in place. They weren't making the noises.

The cries grew louder. Closer.

Shrill warnings.

And then, staring into the distance beyond the platform, I saw them. Small, dark creatures, keeping low, rolling rapidly along the flat ground, tossing their heads back and uttering excited shrieks as they came towards us.

"What are *they*?" Mike cried, moving closer to me.

"Are they wolves?" Dori asked in a trembling voice.

"I hope not!" one of the girls called out.

We all climbed onto the concrete platform and were huddled behind our cases and bags.

The animal cries grew louder as the creatures drew nearer. I could see dozens of them. They scurried towards us over the flat ground as if being blown by the wind.

"Help! Somebody *help* us!" I heard Mike scream.

Next to me, Jay still had two of the red pebbles from his stone-throwing competition in his hand. "Pick up stones!" he was shouting frantically. "Maybe we can scare them away!"

The creatures stopped a few metres from the concrete platform and raised themselves up menacingly on their hind legs.

Huddled between Mike and Jay, I could see them clearly now. They were wolves or wildcats of some sort. Standing upright, they were nearly three feet tall.

They had slender, almost scrawny bodies, covered with spotty red-brown fur. Their paws had long, silvery nails growing out of them. Their heads were nearly as slender as their bodies. Tiny red weasel eyes stared hungrily at us. Their long mouths snapped open and shut, revealing double rows of silvery, daggerlike teeth.

17

"No! No! Help!" Mike dropped to his knees. His whole body convulsed in a shudder of terror.

Some of the kids were crying. Others gaped at the advancing creatures in stunned silence.

I was too scared to cry out or move or do *anything*.

I stared at the row of creatures, my heart thudding, my mouth as dry as cotton wool.

The creatures grew silent. Standing a few metres from the platform, they eyed us, snapping their jaws loudly, hungrily. White froth began to drip from their mouths.

"They—they're going to attack!" a boy yelled.

"They look hungry!" I heard one of the girls say.

The white froth poured thickly over their pointed teeth. They continued to snap their jaws. It sounded like a dozen steel traps being snapped shut.

Suddenly, one of them leapt onto the edge of the platform.

"No!" several kids cried out in unison.

We huddled closer together, trying to stay behind the pile of cases and bags.

Another creature climbed onto the platform. Then three more.

I took a step back.

I saw Jay pull back his arm and heave a red stone at one of the creatures. The stone hit the platform with a *crack* and bounced away.

The creatures weren't frightened. They arched their backs, preparing to attack.

They started making a high-pitched chattering sound.

And moved nearer. Nearer.

Jay threw another stone.

This one hit one of the advancing creatures on the side. It uttered a shrill *eek* of surprise. But it kept moving steadily forward, its red eyes trained on Jay, its jaws snapping hungrily.

"Go away!" Dori cried in a trembling voice. "Go home! Go away! Go *away*!"

But her shouts had no effect.

The creatures advanced.

"Run!" I urged. "Run!"

"We can't outrun *them*!" someone shouted.

The shrill chittering grew louder. Deafening. Until it seemed as if we were surrounded by a wall of sound.

The ugly creatures lowered themselves, ready to pounce.

"Run!" I repeated. "Come on—run!"

My legs wouldn't cooperate. They felt rubbery and weak.

Trying to back away from the attacking creatures, I toppled over backwards off the platform.

I saw flashing stars as the back of my head hit the hard ground.

They're going to get me, I realized.

I can't get away.

19

I heard the sirenlike attack cry.

I heard the scrape of the creatures' long toe-nails over the concrete platform.

I heard the screams and cries of the frightened campers.

Then, as I struggled frantically to pull myself up, I heard the deafening roar.

At first I thought it was an explosion.

I thought the platform had blown up.

But then I turned and saw the rifle.

Another explosion of gunfire. White smoke filled the air.

The creatures spun round and darted away, silent now, their scraggly fur scraping the ground as they kept low, their tails between their furry legs.

"Ha-ha! Look at 'em run!" The man kept the rifle poised on his shoulder as he watched the creatures retreat.

Behind him stood a long green bus.

I pulled myself up and brushed myself off.

Everyone was laughing now, jumping up and down joyfully, celebrating the narrow escape.

I was still too shaken up to celebrate.

"They're running like jackrabbits!" the man declared in a booming voice. He lowered the rifle.

It took me a while to realize he had come out of the camp bus to rescue us. We didn't hear or see the bus pull up because of the attack cries of the animals.

"Are you okay, Mike?" I asked, walking over to my frightened-looking new friend.

"I think so," he replied uncertainly. "I think I'm okay now."

Dawn slapped me on the back, grinning. "We're okay!" she cried. "We're all okay!"

We gathered in front of the man with the rifle.

He was big and red-faced, mostly bald except for a fringe of curly yellow hair around his head. He had a blond moustache under an enormous beak of a nose, and tiny black bird eyes beneath bushy blond eyebrows.

"Hi, kids! I'm Uncle Al. I'm your friendly camp director. I hope you enjoyed that welcome to Camp Nightmoon!" he boomed in a deep voice.

I heard muttered replies.

He leaned the rifle against the bus and took a few steps towards us, studying our faces. He was wearing white shorts and a bright green camp

T-shirt that stretched over his big belly. Two young men, also in green and white, stepped out of the bus, serious expressions on their faces.

"Let's load up," Uncle Al instructed them in his deep voice.

He didn't apologize for being late.

He didn't explain about the weird animals. And he didn't ask if we were okay after that scare.

The two counsellors began dragging the camp trunks and shoving them into the luggage compartment on the bus.

"Looks like a good group this year," Uncle Al shouted. "We'll drop you girls off first across the river. Then we'll get you boys settled in."

"What *were* those awful animals?" Dori called to Uncle Al.

He didn't seem to hear her.

We began climbing onto the bus. I looked for Mike and found him near the end of the line. His face was pale, and he still looked really shaken. "I—I was really scared," he admitted.

"But we're okay," I reassured him. "Now we can relax and have some fun."

"I'm so hungry," Mike complained. "I haven't eaten all day."

One of the counsellors overheard him. "You won't be hungry when you taste the camp food," he told Mike.

We piled into the bus. I sat next to Mike. I could

hear the poor kid's stomach growling. I suddenly realized I was starving, too. And I was really eager to see what Camp Nightmoon looked like. I hoped it wouldn't be a long bus ride to get there.

"How far away is our camp?" I called to Uncle Al, who had slid into the driver's seat.

He didn't seem to hear me.

"Hey, Mike, we're on our way!" I said happily as the bus pulled onto the road.

Mike forced a smile. "I'm so glad to get *away* from there!"

To my surprise, the bus ride took less than five minutes.

We all muttered our shock at what a short trip it was. Why hadn't the first bus taken us all the way?

A big wooden sign proclaiming CAMP NIGHT-MOON came into view, and Uncle Al turned the bus onto a gravel road that led through a patch of short trees into the camp.

We followed the narrow, winding road across the small, brown river. Several small cabins came into view. "Girls' camp," Uncle Al announced. The bus stopped to let the four girls off. Dawn waved to me as she climbed down.

A few minutes later, we pulled into the boys' camp. Through the bus window I could see a row of small, white cabins. On top of a gently sloping hill stood a large, white-tiled building, probably a meeting lodge or refectory.

At the edge of a field, three counsellors, all dressed in white shorts and green T-shirts, were working to start a fire in a large stone barbecue pit.

"Hey, we're going to have a barbecue!" I exclaimed to Mike. I was starting to feel really excited.

Mike smiled, too. He was practically drooling at the thought of food!

The bus came to an abrupt stop at the end of the row of small cabins. Uncle Al pulled himself up quickly from the driver's seat and turned to us. "Welcome to beautiful Camp Nightmoon!" he bellowed. "Step down and line up for your cabin allotments. Once you get unpacked and have dinner, I'll see you at the campfire."

We pushed our way noisily out of the bus. I saw Jay enthusiastically slapping another boy on the back. I think we were all feeling a lot better, forgetting about our earlier experience.

I stepped down and took a deep breath. The cool air smelled really sweet and fresh. I saw a long row of short evergreen trees behind the white lodge on the hill.

As I took my place in the queue, I searched for the riverbank. I could hear the soft rush of the river behind a thick row of evergreens, but I couldn't see it.

Mike, Jay, Colin, and I were assigned to the same cabin. It was Cabin 4. I thought the cabin

24

should have a more interesting name. But it just had a number. Cabin 4.

It was really small, with a low ceiling and windows on both sides. It was just big enough for six campers. There were bunk beds against three walls and tall shelves on the fourth wall, with a little square of space in the middle.

There was no bathroom. I decided it must be in another building.

As the four of us entered the cabin, we saw that one of the beds had already been claimed. It had been carefully made, the green blanket tucked in neatly, some sports magazines and a tape player resting on top.

"That must belong to our counsellor," Jay said, inspecting the tape player.

"Hope we don't have to wear those ugly green T-shirts," Colin said, grinning. He was still wearing his silver sunglasses, even though the sun was nearly down and it was just about as dark as night in the cabin.

Jay claimed a top bunk, and Colin took the bed beneath his.

"Can I have a lower one?" Mike asked me. "I roll around a lot at night. I'm afraid I might fall out of a top one."

"Yeah. Sure. No problem," I replied. I wanted the top bunk anyway. It would be a lot more fun.

"Hope you lot don't snore," Colin said.

"We're not going to sleep in here anyway," Jay

said. "We're going to party all night!" He slapped Mike on the back playfully, but hard enough that Mike went sprawling into the chest of drawers.

"Hey!" Mike whined. "That hurt!"

"Sorry. Suppose I don't know my own strength," Jay replied, grinning at Colin.

The cabin door opened, and a red-haired man with dark freckles all over his face walked in, carrying a big grey plastic bag. He was tall and very skinny and was wearing white shorts and a green camp T-shirt.

"Hey, kids," he said, and dropped the large bag on the cabin floor with a groan. He looked over, then pointed to the bag. "There's your bed stuff," he said. "Make your beds. Try to make them as neat as mine." He pointed to the bunk against the window with the tape player on it.

"Are you our counsellor?" I asked.

He nodded. "Yeah. I'm the lucky one." He turned and started to walk out.

"What's your name?" Jay called after him.

"Larry," he said, pushing open the cabin door. "Your cases will be here in a few minutes," he told us. "You can fight it out over drawer space. Two of the drawers are stuck shut."

He started to leave, then turned back to us. "Keep away from my stuff." The door slammed hard behind him.

26

Peering out of the window, I watched him lope away, taking long, fast strides, bobbing his head as he walked.

"Great guy," Colin muttered sarcastically.

"Really friendly," Jay added, shaking his head.

Then we dived into the plastic bag and pulled out sheets and blankets. Jay and Colin got into a wrestling match over a blanket they claimed was softer than the others.

I tossed a sheet onto my mattress and started to climb up to tuck it in.

I was halfway up the ladder when I heard Mike scream.

Mike was right beneath me, making his bed. He screamed so loud, I cried out and nearly fell off the ladder.

I leapt off the ladder, my heart pounding, and landed beside him.

Staring straight ahead, his mouth wide open in horror, Mike backed away from his bed.

"Mike—what's wrong?" I asked. "What *is* it?"

"S-snakes!" Mike stammered, staring straight ahead at his unmade bed as he backed away.

"Huh?" I followed his gaze. It was too dark to see anything.

Colin laughed. "Not *that* old joke!" he cried.

"Larry put rubber snakes in your bed," Jay said, grinning as he stepped up beside us.

"They're not rubber! They're real!" Mike insisted, his voice trembling.

Jay laughed and shook his head. "I can't believe you fell for that old gag." He took a few steps towards the bed—then stopped. "Hey—!"

I moved close, and the two snakes came into focus. Raising themselves from the shadows, they arched their slender heads, pulling back as if preparing to attack.

"They're real!" Jay cried, turning back to Colin. "Two of them!"

"Probably not poisonous," Colin said, venturing closer.

The snakes let out angry hisses, raising themselves high off the bed. They were very long and skinny. Their heads were wider than their bodies. Their tongues flicked from side to side as they arched themselves menacingly.

"I'm scared of snakes," Mike uttered in a soft voice.

"They're probably scared of you!" Jay joked, slapping Mike on the back.

Mike winced. He was in no mood for Jay's horseplay. "We've got to get Larry or somebody," Mike said.

"No way!" Jay insisted. "You can handle 'em, Mike. There's only two of them!"

Jay gave Mike a playful shove towards the bed. He only meant to give him a scare.

But Mike stumbled—and fell onto the bed.

The snakes darted in unison.

I saw one of them clamp its teeth into Mike's hand.

Mike rose to his feet. He didn't react at first. Then he uttered a high-pitched shriek.

Two drops of blood appeared on the back of his right hand. He stared down at them, then grabbed the hand.

"It *bit* me!" he shrieked.

"Oh, no!" I cried.

"Did it puncture the skin?" Colin asked. "Is it bleeding?"

Jay rushed forward and grabbed Mike's shoulder. "Hey, man—I'm really sorry," he said. "I didn't mean to—"

Mike groaned in pain. "It—really hurts," he whispered. He was breathing really hard, his chest heaving, making weird noises as he breathed.

The snakes, coiled in the middle of his lower bunk, began to hiss again.

"You'd better hurry to the nurse," Jay said, his hand still on Mike's shoulder. "I'll come with you."

"N-no," Mike stammered. His face was as pale as a ghost. He held his hand tightly. "I'll go and find her!" He burst out of the cabin, running at full speed. The door slammed behind him.

"Hey—I didn't mean to push him, you know," Jay explained to us. I could see he was really upset. "I was just joking, just trying to scare him a little. I didn't mean him to fall or anything. . . ." His voice trailed off.

"What are we going to do about *them*?" I asked, pointing at the two coiled snakes.

"I'll get Larry," Colin offered. He started towards the door.

"No, wait." I called him back. "Look. They're sitting on Mike's sheet, right?"

Jay and Colin followed my gaze to the bed. The snakes arched themselves high, preparing to bite again.

"So?" Jay asked, scratching his dishevelled hair.

"So we can wrap them up in the sheet and carry them outside," I said.

Jay stared at me. "Wish I'd thought of that. Let's do it, man!"

"You'll get bitten," Colin warned.

I stared at the snakes. They seemed to be studying me, too. "They can't bite us through the sheet," I said.

"They can try!" Colin exclaimed, hanging back.

"If we're fast enough," I said, taking a cautious step towards the bed, "we can wrap them up before they know what's happening."

The snakes hissed out a warning, drawing themselves higher.

"How did they get in here, anyway?" Colin asked.

"Maybe the camp is *crawling* with snakes," Jay said, grinning. "Maybe you've got some in *your* bed, too, Colin!" He laughed.

"Let's be serious here," I said sternly, my eyes

locked on the coiled snakes. "Are we going to try this or not?"

"Yeah. Let's do it," Jay answered. "I mean, I owe it to Mike."

Colin remained silent.

"I bet I could grab one by the tail and swing him out through the window," Jay said. "You could grab the tail end of the other one and—"

"Let's try my plan first," I suggested quietly.

We crept over to the snakes, sneaking up on them. It was kind of silly since they were staring right at us.

I pointed to one end of the sheet, which was folded up onto the bed. "Grab it there," I instructed Jay. "Then pull it up."

He hesitated. "What if I miss? Or you miss?"

"Then we're in trouble," I replied grimly. My eyes on the snakes, I reached my hand forward to the other corner of the sheet. "Ready? On three," I whispered.

My heart was in my mouth. I could barely choke out, "One, two, three."

At the count of three, we both grabbed for the ends of the sheet.

"Pull!" I cried in a shrill voice I couldn't believe was coming from me.

We pulled up the sheet and brought the ends together, making a bundle.

At the bottom of the bundle, the snakes wriggled frantically. I heard their jaws snap.

They wriggled so hard, the bottom of the bundle swung back and forth.

"They don't like this," Jay said as we hurried to the door, carrying our wriggling, swaying bundle between us, trying to keep our bodies as far away from it as possible.

I pushed open the door with my shoulder, and we ran out onto the grass.

"Now what?" Jay asked.

"Keep going," I replied. I could see one of the snakes poking its head out. "Hurry!"

We ran past the cabins towards a small clump of bushes. Beyond the bushes stood a patch of low trees. When we reached the trees, we swung the bundle back, then heaved the whole sheet into the trees.

It opened as it fell to the ground. The two snakes slithered out instantly and pulled themselves to shelter under the trees.

Jay and I let out loud sighs of relief. We stood there for a moment, hunched over, hands on our knees, trying to catch our breath.

Crouching down, I looked for the snakes. But they had slithered deep into the safety of the evergreens.

I stood up. "I think we should take back Mike's sheet," I said.

"He probably won't want to sleep on it," Jay said. But he reached down and pulled it up from the grass. He bundled it up and tossed it to me.

"It's probably dripping with snake venom," he said, making a disgusted face.

When we got back to the cabin, Colin had made his bed and was busily unpacking the contents of his suitcase, shoving everything into a drawer. He turned as we entered. "How'd it go?" he asked casually.

"Horrible," Jay replied quickly, his expression grim. "We both got bitten. Twice."

"You're a terrible liar!" Colin told him, laughing. "You shouldn't even try."

Jay laughed, too.

Colin turned to me. "You're a hero," he said.

"Thanks for all your help," Jay told him sarcastically.

Colin started to reply. But the cabin door opened, and Larry poked his freckled face in. "How's it going?" he asked. "You're not settled in yet?"

"We had a little problem," Jay told him.

"Where's the fourth boy? The chubby one?" Larry asked, lowering his head so he wouldn't bump it on the doorframe as he stepped inside.

"Mike got bitten. By a snake," I told him.

"There were two snakes in his bed," Jay added.

Larry's expression didn't change. He didn't seem at all surprised. "So where did Mike go?" he asked casually, swatting a mosquito on his arm.

34

"His hand was bleeding. He went to the nurse to get it taken care of," I told him.

"Huh?" Larry's mouth dropped open.

"He went to find the nurse," I repeated.

Larry tossed back his head and started to laugh. "Nurse?" he cried, laughing hard. "*What* nurse?!"

The door opened and Mike returned, still holding his wounded hand. His face was pale, his expression frightened. "They said there *was* no nurse," he told me.

Then he saw Larry perched on top of his bunk. "Larry—my hand," Mike said. He held the hand up so the counsellor could see it. It was stained with bright red blood.

Larry lowered himself to the floor. "I think I have some bandages," he told Mike. He pulled out a slender black case from beneath his bunk and began to search through it.

Mike stood beside him, holding up his hand. Drops of blood splashed on the cabin floor. "They said the camp doesn't have a nurse," Mike repeated.

Larry shook his head. "If you get hurt in *this* camp," he told Mike seriously, "you're on your own."

"I think my hand is swelling up a little," Mike said.

Larry handed him a roll of bandages. "The washroom is at the end of this row of cabins," he told Mike, closing his case and shoving it back under the bed. "Go and wash the hand and bandage it. Hurry. It's almost suppertime."

Holding the bandages tightly in his good hand, Mike hurried off to follow Larry's instructions.

"By the way, how'd you boys get the snakes out of here?" Larry asked, glancing around the cabin.

"We carried them out in Mike's sheet," Jay told him. He pointed at me. "It was Billy's idea."

Larry stared hard at me. "Hey, I'm impressed, Billy," he said. "That was pretty brave, man."

"Maybe I inherited something from my parents," I told him. "They're scientists. Explorers, sort of. They go off for months at a time, exploring the wildest places."

"Well, Camp Nightmoon is pretty wild," Larry said. "And you boys had better be careful. I'm warning you." His expression turned serious. "There's no nurse at Camp Nightmoon. Uncle Al doesn't believe in molly-coddling you boys."

The hot dogs were all charred black but we were so hungry, we didn't care. I wolfed three of them down in less than five minutes. I don't think I'd ever been so hungry in all my life.

The campfire was in a flat clearing surrounded by a circle of round, white stones. Behind us, the large, white-tiled lodge loomed over the sloping hill. Ahead of us a thick line of evergreen trees formed a fence that hid the river from view.

Through a small gap in the trees, I could see a flickering campfire in the distance on the other side of the river. I wondered if that was the campfire of the girls' camp.

I thought about Dawn and Dori. I wondered if the two camps ever got together, if I'd ever see them again.

Dinner around the big campfire seemed to put everyone in a good mood. Jay was the only one sitting near me who complained about the hot dogs being burned. But I think he put away four or five of them anyway!

Mike had trouble eating because of his bandaged hand. When he dropped his first hot dog, I thought he was going to burst into tears. By the end of dinner, he was in a much better mood. His wounded hand had swelled up just a little. But he said it didn't hurt as much as before.

The counsellors were easy to spot. They all wore identical white shorts and green T-shirts. There were eight or ten of them, all young men, probably sixteen or seventeen. They ate together quietly, away from us campers. I kept looking at Larry, but he never once turned round to look at any of us.

I was thinking about Larry, trying to work out if he was shy or if he just didn't like us campers very much. Suddenly, Uncle Al got to his feet and motioned with both hands for us all to be quiet.

"I want to welcome you boys to Camp Nightmoon," he began. "I hope you've all unpacked and are comfortable in your cabins. I know that most of you are first-time campers."

He was speaking quickly, without any pauses between sentences, as if he was running through this for the thousandth time and wanted to get it over with.

"I'd like to tell you some of our basic rules," he continued. "First, lights out is at nine sharp."

A lot of the boys groaned.

"You might think you can ignore this rule," Uncle Al continued, paying no attention to their reaction. "You might think you can sneak out of your cabins to meet or take a walk by the river. But I'm warning you now that we don't allow it, and we have very good ways of making sure this rule is obeyed."

He paused to clear his throat.

Some boys were giggling about something. Opposite from me, Jay burped loudly, which caused more giggles.

Uncle Al didn't seem to hear any of this. "On the other side of the river is the girls' camp," he continued loudly, motioning to the trees. "You might be able to see their campfire. Well, I want to make it clear that swimming or rowing over to the girls' camp is strictly forbidden."

Several boys groaned loudly. This made everyone laugh. Even some of the counsellors laughed. Uncle Al remained grim-faced.

"The woods around Camp Nightmoon are filled with grizzlies and tree bears," Uncle Al continued. "They come to the river to bathe and to drink. And they're usually hungry."

This caused another big reaction from all of us sitting around the fading campfire. Someone made a loud growling sound. Another kid screamed. Then everyone laughed.

"You won't be laughing if a bear claws your head off," Uncle Al said sternly.

He turned to the group of counsellors outside our circle. "Larry, Kurt, come over here," he ordered.

The two counsellors rose obediently to their feet and made their way to the centre of the circle beside Uncle Al.

"I want you two to demonstrate to the new campers the procedure to follow when—er, I mean, *if* you are attacked by a grizzly bear."

Immediately, the two counsellors dropped to the ground on their stomachs. They lay flat and covered the backs of their heads with their hands.

"That's right. I hope you're all paying close attention," the camp director thundered at us. "Cover your neck and head. Try your best not to move." He motioned to the two counsellors. "Thanks, boys. You can get up."

"Have there ever been any bear attacks here?" I called out, cupping my hands so Uncle Al could hear me.

He turned in my direction. "Two last summer," he replied.

Several boys gasped.

"It wasn't pretty," Uncle Al continued. "It's hard to keep still when a huge bear is pawing you and drooling all over you. But if you move..." His voice trailed off, leaving the rest to our imaginations, I suppose.

I felt a cold shiver run down my back. I didn't want to think about bears and bear attacks.

What kind of camp have Mum and Dad sent me to? I found myself wondering. I couldn't wait to phone them and tell them about everything that had happened already.

Uncle Al waited for everyone to be silent, then pointed off to the side. "Do you see that cabin over there?" he asked.

In the dim, evening light, I could make out a cabin standing halfway up the hill towards the lodge. It appeared a little larger than the other cabins. It seemed to be built on a slant, sort of tipping on its side, as if the wind had tried to blow it over.

"I want you to make sure you see that cabin," Uncle Al warned, his voice thundering out above the crackling of the purple fire. "That is known as the Forbidden Cabin. We don't talk about that cabin—and we don't go near it."

I felt another cold shiver as I stared through the grey evening light at the shadowy, tilted cabin. I felt a sharp sting on the back of my neck and slapped a mosquito, too late to keep it from biting me.

"I'm going to repeat what I just said," Uncle Al shouted, still pointing to the dark cabin on the hill. "That is known as the Forbidden Cabin. It has been closed and boarded up for many years. No one is to go near that cabin. *No one.*"

This started everyone talking and laughing. Nervous laughter, I think.

"Why is the Forbidden Cabin forbidden?" someone called out.

"We never talk about it," Uncle Al replied sharply.

Jay leaned over and whispered in my ear, "Let's go and check it out."

I laughed. Then I turned back to Jay uncertainly. "You're kidding—right?"

He grinned in reply and didn't say anything.

I turned back towards the fire. Uncle Al was

wishing us all a good stay and saying how much he was looking forward to camp this year. "And one more rule—" he called out. "You must write to your parents every day. Every day! We want them to know what a great time you're having at Camp Nightmoon."

I saw Mike holding his wounded hand gingerly. "It's starting to throb," he told me, sounding very frightened.

"Maybe Larry has something to put on it," I said. "Let's go and ask him."

Uncle Al dismissed us. We all climbed to our feet, scratching and yawning, and started to make our way in small groups back to the cabins.

Mike and I lingered behind, hoping to talk to Larry. We saw him talking to the other counsellors. He was at least a head taller than all of them.

"Hey, Larry—" Mike called.

But by the time we had pushed our way through the groups of kids heading the other way, Larry had disappeared.

"Maybe he's going to our cabin to make sure we obey lights out," I suggested.

"Let's go and see," Mike replied anxiously.

We walked quickly past the dying campfire. It had stopped crackling but still glowed a deep purple-red. Then we headed along the curve of the hill towards Cabin 4.

"My hand really hurts," Mike groaned, holding it tenderly in front of him. "I'm not just complaining. It's throbbing and it's swelling up. And I'm starting to get the shivers."

"Larry will know what to do," I replied, trying to sound reassuring.

"I hope so," Mike said shakily.

We both stopped when we heard the howls.

Hideous howls. Like an animal in pain. But too human to be from an animal.

Long, shrill howls that cut through the air and echoed down the hill.

Mike uttered a quiet gasp. He turned to me. Even in the darkness, I could see the fright on his face.

"Those cries," he whispered. "They're coming from . . . the Forbidden Cabin!"

A few minutes later, Mike and I trudged into the cabin. Jay and Colin were sitting tensely on their beds. "Where's Larry?" Mike asked, fear creeping into his voice.

"Not here," Colin replied.

"Where *is* he?" Mike demanded shrilly. "I've got to find him. My *hand*!"

"He should be here soon," Jay offered.

I could still hear the strange howls through the open window. "Do you hear that?" I asked, walking over to the window and listening hard.

"Probably a wildcat," Colin said.

"Wildcats don't howl," Mike told him. "Wildcats screech, but they don't howl."

"How do *you* know?" Colin asked, walking over to Larry's bunk and sitting down on the bottom bed.

"We studied them at school," Mike replied.

Another howl made us all stop and listen.

"It sounds like a man," Jay offered, his eyes

45

lighting up excitedly. "A man who's been locked up in the Forbidden Cabin for years and years."

Mike swallowed hard. "Do you really think so?"

Jay and Colin laughed.

"What should I do about my hand?" Mike asked, holding it up. It was definitely swollen.

"Go and wash it again," I told him. "And put a fresh bandage on it." I peered out of the window into the darkness. "Maybe Larry will turn up soon. He probably knows where to get something to put on it."

"I can't believe there isn't a nurse," Mike whined. "Why would my parents send me to a camp where there's no nurse or anything?"

"Uncle Al doesn't like to mollycoddle us," Colin said, echoing Larry's words.

Jay stood up and broke into an imitation of Uncle Al. "Stay away from the Forbidden Cabin!" he cried in a booming deep voice. He sounded a lot like him. "We don't talk about it and we don't ever go near it!"

We all laughed at Jay's impression. Even Mike.

"We should go there tonight!" Colin said enthusiastically. "We should check it out immediately!"

We heard another long, sorrowful howl roll down the hill from the direction of the Forbidden Cabin.

"I—I don't think we should," Mike said softly, examining his hand. He started for the door. "I'm going to go and wash this." The door slammed behind him.

"He's scared," Jay scoffed.

"I'm a bit scared, too," I admitted. "I mean, those awful howls . . ."

Jay and Colin both laughed. "Every camp has something like the Forbidden Cabin. The camp director makes it up," Colin said.

"Yeah," Jay agreed. "Camp directors love scaring kids. It's the only fun they have."

He puffed out his chest and imitated Uncle Al again. "Don't go out after lights out or you'll never be seen again!" he thundered, then burst out laughing.

"There's nothing in that Forbidden Cabin," Colin said, shaking his head. "It's probably completely empty. It's all just a joke. You know. Like camp ghost stories. Every camp has its own ghost story."

"How do you know?" I asked, dropping down onto Mike's bed. "Have you been to camp before?"

"No," Colin replied. "But I have friends who've told me about *their* camp." He reached up and pulled off his silver sunglasses for the first time. He had bright sky-blue eyes, like big blue marbles.

We suddenly heard the sound of a bugle,

47

repeating a slow, sad-sounding tune.

"That must be the signal for lights out," I said, yawning. I started to pull off my shoes. I was too tired to change or wash. I planned to sleep in my clothes.

"Let's sneak out and explore the Forbidden Cabin," urged Jay. "Come on. We can be the first ones to do it!"

I yawned again. "I'm really too tired," I told him.

"Me, too," Colin said. He turned to Jay. "How about tomorrow night?"

Jay's face fell in disappointment.

"Tomorrow," Colin insisted, kicking his shoes into the corner and starting to pull off his socks.

"I wouldn't do it if I were you!"

The voice startled all three of us. We turned to the window where Larry's head suddenly appeared from out of the darkness. He grinned in at us. "I'd listen to Uncle Al if I were you," he said.

How long had he been out there listening to us? I wondered. Was he deliberately *spying* on us?

The door opened. Larry lowered his head as he loped in. His grin had faded. "Uncle Al wasn't messing around," he said seriously.

"Yeah. Sure," Colin replied sarcastically. He climbed up to his bed and slid beneath the wool blanket.

"I suppose the camp ghost will get us if we go out after lights out," Jay joked, tossing a towel across the room.

"No. No ghost," Larry said softly. "But Sabre will." He pulled out his drawer and began searching for something inside it.

"Huh? Who's Sabre?" I asked, suddenly wide awake.

"Sabre is an *it*," Larry answered mysteriously.

"Sabre is a red-eyed monster who eats a camper every night," Colin sneered. He stared down at me. "There *is* no Sabre. Larry's just giving us another phony camp story."

Larry stopped searching his drawer and gazed up at Colin. "No, I'm not," he insisted in a low voice. "I'm trying to save you boys some trouble. I'm not trying to scare you."

"Then what is Sabre?" I asked impatiently.

Larry pulled a sweater from the drawer, then pushed the drawer shut. "You don't want to find out," he replied.

"Come on. Tell us what it is," I begged.

"He isn't going to," Colin said.

"I'll tell you boys only one thing. Sabre will rip your heart out," Larry said flatly.

Jay sniggered. "Yeah. Sure."

"I'm serious!" Larry snapped. "I'm not kidding!" He pulled the sweater over his head. "You don't believe me? Go out one night. Go out and meet Sabre." He struggled to get his arm into the sweater sleeve. "But before you do," he warned, "leave me a note with your address so I'll know where to send your belongings."

We had fun the next morning.

We all woke up really early. The sun was just rising over the horizon to the south, and the air was still cool and damp. I could hear birds chirping.

The sound reminded me of home. As I lowered myself to the floor and stretched, I thought of my mum and dad and wished I could phone them and tell them about the camp. But it was only the second day. I'd be too embarrassed to phone them on the second day.

I was definitely homesick. But luckily there wasn't any time to feel sad. After we pulled on fresh clothes, we hurried up to the lodge on the hill, which served as a meeting hall, theatre, and refectory.

Long tables and benches were set up in straight rows in the centre of the enormous room. The floorboards and walls were all dark redwood. Redwood ceiling beams crisscrossed high above our heads. There were no windows, so it felt as if we were in an enormous, dark cave.

The clatter of dishes and cups and cutlery was deafening. Our shouts and laughter rang off the high ceiling, echoed off the hardwood walls. Mike shouted something to me from across the table, but I couldn't hear him because of the racket.

Some boys complained about the food, but I thought it was okay. We had scrambled eggs, bacon strips, fried potatoes, and toast, with tall cups of orange juice. I never eat a breakfast that big at home. But I found that I was really starving, and I gobbled it up.

After breakfast we lined up outside the lodge to form different activity groups. The sun had climbed high in the sky. It was going to be really hot. Our excited voices echoed off the sloping hill. We were all laughing and talking, feeling good.

Larry and two other counsellors, clipboards in hand, stood in front of us, shielding their eyes from the bright sun as they divided us into groups. The first group of about ten boys headed off to the river for a morning swim.

Some people have all the luck, I thought. I was eager to get to the riverbank and see what the river was like.

As I waited for my name to be called, I spotted a pay phone on the wall of the lodge. My parents flashed into my mind again. Maybe I *will* call them later, I decided. I was so eager to describe the camp to them and tell them about my new friends.

"Okay, boys. Follow me to the ball field," Larry instructed us. "We're going to play our first game of scratchball."

About twelve of us, including everyone from my cabin, followed Larry down the hill towards the flat grassy area that formed the playing field.

I jogged to catch up with Larry, who always seemed to walk at top speed, stretching out his long legs as if he were in a terrible hurry. "Are we going to swim after this?" I asked.

Without slowing his pace, he glanced at his clipboard. "Yeah, I suppose so," he replied. "You boys'll need a swim. We're going to work up a sweat."

"You ever play scratchball before?" Jay asked me as we hurried to keep up with Larry.

"Yeah. Of course," I replied. "We play it a lot at school."

Larry stopped at the far corner of the wide, green field, where the bases and batter's square had already been set up. He made us line up and divided us into two teams.

Scratchball is an easy game to learn. The batter throws the ball in the air as high and as far as he can. Then he has to run round the bases before someone on the other team catches the ball, tags him with it, or throws him out.

Larry started calling out names, dividing us into teams. But when he called out Mike's name, Mike stepped up to Larry, holding his bandaged hand tenderly. "I—I don't think I can play, Larry," Mike stammered.

"Come on, Mike. Don't whine," Larry snapped.

"But it really hurts," Mike insisted. "It's throbbing like mad, Larry. The pain is shooting all the way up and down my side. And, look"— he raised the hand to Larry's face—"It's all swollen up!"

Larry pushed the arm away gently with his clipboard. "Go and sit in the shade," he told Mike.

"Shouldn't I get some medicine or something to put on it?" Mike asked shrilly. I could see the poor boy was really in a bad way.

"Just sit over there by that tree," Larry ordered, pointing to a clump of short, leafy trees at the edge of the field. "We'll talk about it later."

Larry turned away from Mike and blew a whistle to start the game. "I'll take Mike's place on the Blue team," he announced, jogging onto the field.

I forgot about Mike as soon as the game got underway. We were having a lot of fun. Most of the boys were pretty good scratchball players, and we played much faster than my friends do back home in the playground.

My first time up at the batter's square, I heaved the ball really high. But it dropped right into a fielder's hands, and I was out. My second time up, I made it to three bases before I was tagged out.

Larry was a great player. When he came up to the batter's square, he tossed the ball harder than I've ever seen anyone toss it. It sailed over the fielders' heads and, as they chased after it, Larry rounded all the bases, his long legs stretching out gracefully as he ran.

By the fourth inning, our team, the Blue team, was ahead twelve to six. We had all played hard and were really hot and sweaty. I was looking forward to that swim at the riverbank.

Colin was on the Red team. I noticed that he was the only player who wasn't enjoying the game. He had been tagged out twice, and he'd missed an easy catch in the field.

I realized that Colin wasn't very athletic. He had long, skinny arms without any muscles, and he also ran awkwardly.

In the third inning Colin got into an argument with a player on my team about whether a toss had been foul or not. A few minutes later, Colin argued angrily with Larry about a ball that he claimed should have been out.

He and Larry shouted at each other for a few

minutes. It was no big deal, a typical sporting argument. Larry finally ordered Colin to shut up and get back to the outfield. Colin grudgingly obeyed, and the game continued.

I didn't think about it again. I mean, that kind of arguing happens all the time in ball games. And there are boys who enjoy the arguments as much as the game.

But then, in the next inning, something strange happened that gave me a really bad feeling and made me stop and wonder just what was going on.

Colin's team came to bat. Colin stepped up to the batter's square and prepared to toss the ball.

Larry was playing the outfield. I was standing nearby, also in the field.

Colin tossed the ball high, but not very far.

Larry and I both came running in to get it.

Larry got there first. He picked up the small, hard ball on the first bounce, drew back his arm—and then I saw his expression change.

I saw his features tighten in anger. I saw his eyes narrow, his copper-coloured eyebrows lower in concentration.

With a loud grunt of effort, Larry heaved the ball as hard as he could.

It struck Colin in the back of the head, making a loud *crack* sound as it hit.

Colin's silver sunglasses went flying through the air.

Colin stopped short and uttered a short, high-pitched cry. His arms flew up as if he'd been shot. Then his knees buckled.

He collapsed in a heap, face-down on the grass. He didn't move.

The ball rolled away over the grass.

I cried out in shock.

Then I saw Larry's expression change again. His eyes opened wide in disbelief. His mouth dropped open in horror.

"No!" he cried. "It slipped! I didn't mean to throw it at him!"

I knew Larry was lying. I had seen the anger on his face before he threw the ball.

I sank down to my knees on the ground as Larry went running towards Colin. I felt dizzy and upset and confused. I had a sick feeling in my stomach.

"The ball slipped!" Larry was yelling. "It just slipped."

Liar, I thought. Liar. Liar. Liar.

I forced myself up on my feet and hurried to join the circle of boys around Colin. When I got there, Larry was kneeling over Colin, raising Colin's head off the ground gently with both hands.

Colin's eyes were open wide. He stared up at Larry groggily, and uttered low moans.

"Give him room," Larry was shouting. "Give him room." He gazed down at Colin.

"The ball slipped. I'm really sorry. The ball slipped."

Colin moaned. His eyes rolled around in his head. Larry pulled off Colin's red bandanna and mopped Colin's forehead with it.

Colin moaned again. His eyes closed.

"Help me carry him to the lodge," Larry instructed two kids from the Red team. "The rest of you boys get changed for your swim. The riverbank counsellor will be waiting for you."

I watched as Larry and the two boys hoisted Colin up and started to carry him towards the lodge. Larry gripped him under the shoulders. The two boys awkwardly took hold of his legs.

The sick feeling in my stomach hadn't gone away. I kept remembering the intense expression of anger on Larry's face as he'd heaved the ball at the back of Colin's head.

I knew it had been deliberate.

I started to follow them. I don't know why. I suppose I was so upset, I wasn't thinking clearly.

They were nearly at the bottom of the hill when I saw Mike catch up with them. He ran alongside Larry, holding his swollen hand.

"Can I come, too?" Mike pleaded. "Someone has to look at my hand. It's really bad, Larry. Please—can I come, too?"

"Yeah. You'd better," I heard Larry reply curtly.

Good, I thought. Finally someone was going to pay some attention to Mike's snakebite wound.

Ignoring the sweat pouring down my forehead, I watched them make their way up the hill to the lodge.

This shouldn't have happened, I thought, suddenly feeling shivery despite the hot sun.

Something is wrong. Something is terribly wrong here.

How was I to know that the horrors were just beginning . . .

Later that afternoon, Jay and I were writing letters to our parents. I was feeling pretty upset about things. I kept seeing the angry expression on Larry's face as he'd heaved the ball at the back of Colin's head.

I wrote about it in my letter, and I also told my mum and dad about how there was no nurse there, and about the Forbidden Cabin.

Jay stopped writing and looked up at me from his bunk. He was really sunburned. His cheeks and forehead were bright red.

He scratched his red hair. "We're dropping like flies," he said, gesturing around the nearly empty cabin.

"Yeah," I agreed wistfully. "I hope Colin and Mike are okay." And then I blurted out, "Larry deliberately hit Colin."

"Huh?" Jay stopped scratching his hair and lowered his hand to the bunk. "He *what*?"

"He deliberately threw the ball at Colin's

60

head. I *saw* him," I said, my voice shaky. I wasn't going to tell anyone, but now I was glad I had. It made me feel a little bit better to get it out.

But then I saw that Jay didn't believe me. "That's impossible," he said quietly. "Larry's our counsellor. His hand slipped. That's all."

I started to argue when the cabin door opened and Colin entered, with Larry at his side.

"Colin! How *are* you?" I cried. Jay and I both jumped up.

"Not bad," Colin replied. He forced a thin smile. I couldn't see his eyes. They were hidden once again behind his silver sunglasses.

"He's still a little wobbly, but he's okay," Larry said cheerfully, holding Colin's arm.

"I'm sort of seeing double," Colin admitted. "I mean, this cabin looks really crowded to me. There are two of each of you."

Jay and I uttered short, uncomfortable laughs.

Larry helped Colin over to the lower bunk where Jay had been sitting. "He'll be just fine in a day or two," Larry told us.

"Yeah. The headache is a little better already," Colin said, gently rubbing the back of his head, then lying down on top of the bedcovers.

"Did you see a doctor?" I asked.

"No. Just Uncle Al," Colin replied. "He looked it over and said I'd be fine."

I cast a suspicious glance at Larry, but he turned his back on us and crouched down to search for something in the duffel bag he kept under his bed.

"Where's Mike? Is he okay?" Jay asked Larry.

"Uh-huh," Larry answered without turning round. "He's fine."

"But where is he?" I demanded.

Larry shrugged. "Still at the lodge, I suppose. I don't really know."

"But is he coming back?" I insisted.

Larry shoved the bag under his bed and stood up. "Have you two finished your letters?" he asked. "Hurry up and get changed for dinner. You can post your letters at the lodge."

He started for the door. "Hey, don't forget tonight is Tent Night. You boys are sleeping in a tent tonight."

We all groaned. "But, Larry, it's so cold out!" Jay protested.

Larry ignored him and turned away.

"Hey, Larry, do you have anything I can put on this sunburn?" Jay called after him.

"No," Larry replied and disappeared out of the door.

Jay and I helped Colin up to the lodge. He was still seeing double, and his headache was pretty bad.

The three of us sat at the end of the long table nearest the window. A strong breeze blew cool air over the table, which felt good on our sunburned skin.

We had some kind of meat with potatoes and gravy for dinner. It wasn't great, but I was so hungry, it didn't matter. Colin didn't have much appetite. He picked at the edges of his grey meat.

The refectory was as noisy as ever. Kids were laughing and shouting to friends across the long tables. At one table, boys were throwing breadsticks back and forth like javelins.

As usual, the counsellors, dressed in their green and white, ate together at a table in the far corner and ignored us campers completely.

The rumour spread that we were going to learn all of the camp songs after dinner. Boys were groaning and complaining about that.

About halfway through dinner, Jay and the boy across the table, a boy called Roger, started horsing around, trying to wrestle a breadstick from each other. Jay pulled hard and won the breadstick—and spilled his entire cup of grape juice on my shorts.

"Hey!" I jumped up angrily, staring down as the purple stain spread across the front of my shorts.

"Billy had an accident!" Roger cried out. And everyone laughed.

"Yeah. He purpled in his pants!" Jay added.

Everyone thought that was hilarious. Someone threw a breadstick at me. It bounced off my chest and landed on my dinner plate. More laughter.

The food fight lasted only a few minutes. Then two of the counsellors broke it up. I decided I'd better run back to the cabin and change my shorts. As I hurried out, I could hear Jay and Roger calling out jokes about me.

I ran full-speed down the hill towards the cabins. I wanted to get back up to the refectory in time for dessert.

Pushing open the cabin door with my shoulder, I darted across the small room to the chest of drawers and pulled open my drawer.

"Huh?"

To my surprise, I stared into an empty drawer. It had been completely cleaned out.

"What's going on here?" I asked aloud. "Where's my stuff?"

Confused, I took a step back—and realized I had opened the wrong drawer. This wasn't my drawer.

It was Mike's.

I stared for a long time into the empty drawer.

Mike's clothes had all been removed. I turned and looked for his suitcase, which had been stacked on its side behind our bunk.

Mike's suitcase had gone, too.

Mike wasn't coming back.

I was so upset, I ran back to the refectory without changing my shorts.

Panting loudly, I made my way to the counsellors' table and came up behind Larry. He was talking to the counsellor next to him, a fat guy with long, straggly blond hair. "Larry—Mike's gone!" I cried breathlessly.

Larry didn't turn round. He kept talking to the other counsellor as if I weren't there.

I grabbed Larry's shoulder. "Larry—listen!" I cried. "Mike—he's gone!"

Larry turned round slowly, his expression annoyed. "Go back to your table, Billy," he snapped. "This table is for counsellors only."

"But what about Mike?" I insisted shrilly. "His stuff has gone. What's happened to him? Is he okay?"

"How should I know?" Larry replied impatiently.

"Did they send him home?" I asked, refusing to back away until I had some kind of an answer.

"Yeah. Maybe." Larry shrugged and lowered his gaze. "You spilled something on your shorts."

My heart was pounding so hard, I could feel the blood pulsing at my temples. "You really don't know what happened to Mike?" I asked, feeling defeated.

Larry shook his head. "I'm sure he's fine," he replied, turning back to his pals.

"He probably went for a swim," the straggly-haired guy next to him sniggered.

Larry and some of the other counsellors laughed, too.

I didn't think it was funny. I felt pretty sick. And more than a little frightened.

Don't the counsellors at this camp care what happens to us? I asked myself glumly.

I made my way back to the table. They were passing round chocolate pudding for dessert, but I wasn't hungry.

I told Colin, and Jay, and Roger about Mike's drawer being cleaned out, and about how Larry had pretended he didn't know anything about it. They didn't get as upset about it as I was.

"Uncle Al probably had to send Mike home because of his hand," Colin said quietly, spooning up his pudding. "It was pretty swollen."

"But why wouldn't Larry tell me the truth?" I asked, my stomach still feeling as if I had eaten a giant rock for dinner. "Why did he say he didn't know what had happened to Mike?"

"Counsellors don't like to talk about these things," Jay said, slapping the top of his pudding with his spoon. "It might give us poor little kids nightmares." He filled his spoon with pudding, tilted it back, and flung a dark gob of pudding onto Roger's forehead.

"Jay—you're dead meat now!" Roger cried, plunging his spoon into the chocolate goo. He shot a gob of it onto the front of Jay's sleeveless T-shirt.

66

That started a pudding war that spread down the long table.

There was no more talk about Mike.

After dinner, Uncle Al talked about Tent Night and what a great time we were going to have sleeping in tents tonight. "Just be very quiet so the bears can't find you!" he joked. Some joke!

Then he and the counsellors taught us the camp songs. Uncle Al made us sing them over and over again until we had learned them off by heart.

I didn't feel much like singing. But Jay and Roger began making up really gross words to the songs. And pretty soon, most of us had joined in, singing our own versions of the songs as loudly as we could.

Later, we were all making our way down the hill towards our tents. It was a cool, clear night. A wash of pale stars covered the purple-black sky.

I helped Colin down the hill. He was still seeing double and feeling a little weak.

Jay and Roger walked a few steps ahead of us, shoving each other with their shoulders, first to the left, then to the right.

Suddenly, Jay turned back to Colin and me. "Tonight's the night," he whispered, a devilish grin spreading across his face.

"Huh? Tonight's *what* night?" I demanded.

"Ssshhh." He raised a finger to his lips. "When everyone's asleep, Roger and I are going to go and explore the Forbidden Cabin." He turned to Colin. "You with us?"

Colin shook his head sadly. "I don't think I can, Jay."

Walking backwards in front of us, Jay locked his eyes on mine. "How about you, Billy? You coming?"

"I—I think I'll stay with Colin," I told him.

I heard Roger mutter something about me being a chicken. Jay looked disappointed. "You're going to miss out," he said.

"That's okay. I'm pretty tired," I said. It was true. I felt so weary after this long day, every muscle ached. Even my hair hurt!

Jay and Roger made whispered plans all the way back to the tent.

At the bottom of the hill, I stopped and gazed up at the Forbidden Cabin. It appeared to lean towards me in the pale starlight. I listened for the familiar howls that seemed to come from inside it. But tonight there was only a heavy silence.

The large plastic tents were lined up in the cabin area. I crawled into ours and lay down on top of my sleeping bag. The ground was really hard. I could see this was going to be a long night.

Jay and Colin were messing around with their sleeping bags at the back of the tent. "It seems weird without Mike here," I said, feeling a sudden chill.

"Now you'll have more room to put your stuff," Jay replied casually. He sat hunched against the tent wall, his expression tense, his eyes on the darkness outside the tent door, which was left open a few centimetres.

Larry was nowhere to be seen. Colin sat quietly. He still wasn't feeling right.

I shifted my weight and stretched out, trying to find a comfortable position. I really wanted to go to sleep. But I knew I wouldn't be able to sleep until Jay and Roger had returned from their adventure.

Time moved slowly. It was cold outside, and the air was heavy and wet inside the tent.

I stared up at the dark plastic tent walls. An insect crawled across my forehead. I squashed it with my hand.

I could hear Jay and Colin whispering behind me, but I couldn't make out their words. Jay sniggered nervously.

I must have dozed off. An insistent whispering sound woke me up. It took me a while to realize it was someone whispering outside the tent.

I lifted my head and saw Roger's face peering in. I sat up, alert.

"Wish us luck," Jay whispered.

"Good luck," I whispered back, my voice clogged from sleep.

In the darkness I saw Jay's large, shadowy form crawl quickly to the tent door. He pushed it open, revealing a square of purple sky, then vanished into the darkness.

I shivered. "Let's sneak back to the cabin," I whispered to Colin. "It's too cold out here. And the ground feels like solid rock."

Colin agreed. We both scrambled out of the tent and made our way silently to our nice, warm cabin. Inside, we headed for the window to try to see Jay and Roger.

"They're going to get caught," I whispered. "I just know it."

"They won't get caught," Colin disagreed. "But they won't see anything, either. There's nothing to see up there. It's just a stupid cabin."

Poking my head out of the window, I could hear Jay and Roger giggling quietly out somewhere in the dark. The camp was so silent, so eerily silent. I could hear their whispers, their legs brushing through the tall grass.

"They'd better be quiet," Colin muttered, leaning against the window frame. "They're making too much noise."

"They must be up to the hill by now," I whispered. I stuck my head out as far as I could, but I couldn't see them.

71

Colin started to reply, but the first scream made him stop.

It was a scream of horror that cut through the silent air.

"Oh!" I cried out and pulled my head in.

"Was that Jay or Roger?" Colin asked, his voice trembling.

The second scream was more terrifying than the first.

Before it had died down, I heard animal snarls. Loud and angry. Like an eruption of thunder.

Then I heard Jay's desperate plea: "Help us! Please—somebody help us!"

My heart thudding in my chest, I lurched to the cabin door and pulled it open. The hideous screams still ringing in my ears, I plunged out into the darkness, the dew-covered ground soaking my bare feet.

"Jay—where are you?" I heard myself calling, but I didn't recognize my shrill, frightened voice.

And then I saw a dark form running towards me, running bent over, arms outstretched.

"Jay!" I cried. "What—*is* it? What *happened*?"

He ran up to me, still bent forward, his face twisted in horror, his eyes wide and unblinking. His bushy hair appeared to stand straight up.

"It—it got Roger," he moaned, his chest heaving as he struggled to straighten up.

"What did?" I demanded.

"What was it?" Colin asked, right behind me.

"I—I don't know!" Jay stammered, shutting his eyes tight. "It—it tore Roger to pieces."

Jay uttered a loud sob. Then he opened his eyes and spun around in terror. "Here it comes!" he shrieked. "Now it's coming after *us*!"

In the pale starlight, I saw Jay's eyes roll up in his head. His knees collapsed, and he began to slump to the ground.

I grabbed him before he fell and dragged him into the cabin. Colin slammed the door behind us.

Once inside, Jay recovered slowly. The three of us froze in place and listened hard. I was still holding onto Jay's heaving shoulders. He was as white as a sheet, and his breath came out in short, frightened moans.

We listened.

Silence.

The air hung hot and still.

Nothing moved.

No footsteps. No animal approaching.

Just Jay's frightened moans and the pounding of my heart.

And then, somewhere far in the distance, I heard the howl. Soft and low at first, then rising on the wind. A howl that chilled my blood and made me cry out.

"It's Sabre!"

"*Don't let it get me!*" Jay shrieked, covering his face with his hands. He dropped to his knees on the cabin floor. "Don't let it get me!"

I raised my eyes to Colin, who was huddled against the wall, away from the window. "We have to get Larry," I managed to choke out. "We have to get help."

"But how?" Colin demanded in a trembling voice.

"*Don't let it get me!*" Jay repeated, crumpled on the floor.

"It isn't coming here," I told him, trying to sound certain, trying to sound soothing. "We're okay inside the cabin, Jay. It isn't coming here."

"But it got Roger and—" Jay started. His entire body convulsed in a shudder of terror.

Thinking about Roger, I felt a stab of fear in my chest.

Was it really true? Was it true that Roger had been attacked by some kind of creature? That he'd been slashed to pieces?

I'd heard the screams from the hillside. Two bloodcurdling screams.

They'd been so loud, so horrifying. Hadn't anyone else in the camp heard them, too? Hadn't any other kids heard Roger's cries? Hadn't any counsellors heard?

I froze in place and listened.

Silence. The whisper of the breeze rustling the tree leaves.

No voices. No cries of alarm. No hurried footsteps.

I turned back towards the others. Colin had helped Jay to his bunk. "Where can Larry be?" Colin asked. His eyes, for once not hidden behind the silver sunglasses, showed real fear.

"Where can *everyone* be?" I asked, crossing my arms over my chest and starting to pace back and forth in the small space between the beds. "There isn't a sound out there."

I saw Jay's eyes go wide with horror. He was staring at the open window. "The creature—" he cried. "Here it comes! It's coming through the window!"

All three of us gaped in horror at the open window.

But no creature jumped in.

As I stared, frozen in the middle of the cabin, I could see only darkness and a fringe of pale stars.

Outside in the trees, crickets started up a shrill clatter. There was no other sound.

Poor Jay was so frightened and upset, he was seeing things.

Somehow Colin and I got him a little calmed down. We made him take off his shoes and lie down on the lower bed. And we covered him up with three blankets to help him to stop trembling.

Colin and I wanted to run for help. But we were too frightened to go outside.

The three of us were up all night. Larry never appeared.

Except for the crickets and the brush of the

wind through the trees, the camp was silent.

I think I must have finally dozed off just before dawn. I had strange nightmares about fires and people trying to run away.

I was woken by Colin shaking me hard. "Breakfast," he said hoarsely. "Hurry. We're late."

I sat up groggily. "Where's Larry?"

"He never showed up," Colin replied, motioning to Larry's unused bunk.

"We've got to find him! We've got to tell him what happened!" Jay cried, hurrying to the cabin door with his trainers untied.

Colin and I stumbled after him, both of us only half-awake. It was a cool, grey morning. The sun was trying hard to poke through high white clouds.

The three of us stopped halfway up the hill to the refectory. Reluctantly, our eyes searched the ground around the Forbidden Cabin.

I don't know what I expected to see. But there was no sign of Roger.

No sign of any struggle. No dried blood on the ground. The tall grass wasn't bent or matted down.

"Weird," I heard Jay mutter, shaking his head. "That's weird."

I tugged his arm to get him moving, and we hurried the rest of the way up to the lodge.

The refectory was as noisy as ever. Kids were

laughing and shouting to each other. It all seemed perfectly normal. I guessed that no one had made an announcement about Roger yet.

Some kids called to Colin and me. But we ignored them and searched for Roger, moving quickly through the aisles between the tables.

No sign of him.

I had a heavy, queasy feeling in my stomach as we hurried to the counsellors' table in the corner.

Larry glanced up from a big plate of scrambled eggs and bacon as the three of us advanced on him.

"What happened to Roger?"

"Is he okay?"

"Where were you last night?"

"Roger and I were attacked."

"We were afraid to go and find you."

All three of us bombarded Larry at once.

His face was filled with confusion, and he raised both hands to silence us. "Whoa," he said. "Calm down, boys. What are you talking about?"

"About Roger!" Jay screamed, his face turning bright red. "The creature—it jumped on him. And—and—"

Larry glanced at the other counsellors at the table, who looked as confused as he did. "Creature? What creature?" Larry demanded.

"It attacked Roger!" Jay screamed. "It was coming after me and—"

Larry stared up at Jay. "Someone was attacked? I don't think so, Jay." He turned to the counsellor next to him, a pudgy guy called Derek. "Did you hear anything in your area?"

Derek shook his head.

"Isn't Roger in your group?" Larry asked Derek.

Derek shook his head. "Not in *my* group."

"But Roger—!" Jay insisted.

"We didn't get any report about any attack," Larry said, interrupting. "If a camper had been attacked by a bear or anything, we'd hear about it."

"And we'd hear the noise," Derek offered. "You know. Screams or something."

"I heard screams," I told them.

"We both heard screams," Colin added quickly. "And Jay came running back, crying for help."

"Well, why didn't anyone else hear it?" Larry demanded, turning his gaze on Jay. His expression changed. "Where did this happen? When?" he asked suspiciously.

Jay's face darkened to a deeper red. "After lights out," he admitted. "Roger and I went up to the Forbidden Cabin, and—"

"Are you sure it wasn't a bear?" Derek interrupted. "Some bears were spotted downriver yesterday afternoon."

"It was a *creature!*" Jay screamed angrily.

"You shouldn't have been out," Larry said, shaking his head.

"Why won't you listen to me?" Jay screamed. "Roger was attacked. This big thing jumped on him and—"

"We would've heard something," Derek said calmly, glancing at Larry.

"Yeah," Larry agreed. "The counsellors were all up here at the lodge. We would've heard any screams."

"But, Larry—you've got to check it out!" I cried. "Jay isn't making it up. It really happened!"

"Okay, okay," Larry replied, raising his hands as if surrendering. "I'll go and ask Uncle Al about it, okay?"

"Hurry," Jay insisted. "Please!"

"I'll ask Uncle Al after breakfast," Larry said, turning back to his eggs and bacon. "I'll see you boys at morning swim later. I'll report what Uncle Al says."

"But, Larry—" Jay pleaded.

"I'll ask Uncle Al," Larry said firmly. "If anything happened last night, he'll know about it." He raised a piece of bacon to his mouth and chewed on it. "I think you've just had a bad nightmare or something," he continued, eyeing Jay suspiciously. "But I'll let you know what Uncle Al says."

"It wasn't a nightmare!" Jay cried shrilly.

Larry turned his back on us and continued eating his breakfast. "Don't you *care*?" Jay screamed at him. "Don't you *care* what happens to us?"

I saw that a lot of kids had stopped eating their breakfast to gawp at us. I pulled Jay away, and tried to get him to go to our table. But he insisted on searching the entire refectory again. "I know Roger *isn't* here," he insisted. "He—he *can't* be!"

For the second time, the three of us made our way up and down the aisles between the tables, studying every face.

One thing was for sure: Roger was nowhere to be seen.

The sun burned through the high clouds just as we reached the riverbank for morning swim. The air was still cool. The thick, leafy bushes along the riverbank glistened wetly in the white glare of sunlight.

I dropped my towel under a bush and turned to the gently flowing green water. "I bet it's cold this morning," I said to Colin, who was retying the string on his swimming trunks.

"I just want to go back to the bunk and go to sleep," Colin said, plucking at a knot. He wasn't seeing double any longer, but he was tired from being up all night.

Several boys were already wading into the river. They were complaining about the cold water, splashing each other, shoving each other forward.

"Where's Larry?" Jay demanded breathlessly, pushing his way through the clump of bushes to get to us. His auburn hair was a mess, half of it standing straight up on the side of his head. His eyes were red-rimmed and bloodshot.

"Where's Larry? He promised he'd be here," Jay said, frantically searching the waterfront.

"Here I am." The three of us spun round as Larry appeared from the bushes behind us. He was wearing baggy green Camp Nightmoon swimming trunks.

"Well?" Jay demanded. "What did Uncle Al say? About Roger?"

Larry's expression was serious. His eyes locked on Jay's. "Uncle Al and I went all around the Forbidden Cabin," he told Jay. "There wasn't any attack there. There couldn't have been."

"But it—it got Roger," Jay cried shrilly. "It slashed him. I saw it!"

Larry shook his head, his eyes still burning into Jay's. "That's the other thing," he said softly. "Uncle Al and I went up to the office and checked the records, Jay. And there *is* no camper here this year called Roger. Not a first name or a middle name. No Roger. No Roger at all."

Jay's mouth dropped open and he uttered a low gasp.

The three of us stared in disbelief at Larry, letting his startling news sink in.

"Someone's made a mistake," Jay said finally, his voice trembling with emotion. "We searched the refectory for him, Larry. And he's gone. Roger isn't here."

"He never *was* here," Larry said without any emotion at all.

"I—I just don't believe this!" Jay cried.

"How about a swim, boys?" Larry said, motioning to the water.

"Well, what do *you* think?" I demanded of Larry. I couldn't believe he was being so calm about this. "What do *you* think happened last night?"

Larry shrugged. "I don't know what to think," he replied, his eyes on a cluster of swimmers farthest from the shore. "Maybe you boys are trying to pull a weird joke on me."

"Huh? Is *that* what you think?" Jay cried. "That it's a *joke*?!"

Larry shrugged again. "Swim time, boys. Get some exercise, okay?"

Jay started to say more, but Larry quickly turned and went running into the green water. He took four or five running steps off the shore, then dived in, pulling himself quickly through the water, taking long, steady strokes.

"I'm not going in," Jay insisted angrily. "I'm going back to the cabin." His face was bright red. His chin was trembling. I could see that he was about to cry. He turned and began running through the bushes, dragging his towel along the ground.

"Hey, wait up!" Colin went running after him.

I stood there trying to decide what to do. I didn't want to follow Jay to the cabin. There wasn't anything I could do to help him.

Maybe a cold swim will make me feel better, I thought.

Maybe *nothing* will make me feel better, I told myself glumly.

I stared out at the other boys in the water. Larry and another counsellor were setting up a race. I could hear them discussing what kind of stroke should be used.

They all seem to be having a great time, I thought, watching them line up.

So why aren't I?

Why have I been so frightened and unhappy since I arrived here? Why don't the other campers see how weird and frightening this place is?

I shook my head, unable to answer my questions.

I need a swim, I decided.

I took a step towards the water.

But someone reached out from the bushes and grabbed me roughly from behind.

I started to scream out in protest.

But my attacker quickly clamped a hand over my mouth to silence me.

I tried to pull away, but I'd been caught off guard.

As the hands tugged me, I lost my balance and I was pulled back into the bushes.

Is this a joke? What's going on? I wondered.

Suddenly, as I tried to tug myself free, the hands let go.

I went sailing headfirst into a clump of fat green leaves.

It took me a long moment to pull myself up. Then I spun round to face my attacker.

"Dawn!" I cried.

"Ssshhhh!" She leapt forward and clamped a hand over my mouth again. "Duck down," she whispered urgently. "They'll see you."

I obediently ducked behind the low bush. She let go of me again and moved back. She was wearing a blue, one-piece bathing suit. It was wet. Her blonde hair was also wet, dripping down onto her bare shoulders.

"Dawn—what are you *doing* here?" I whispered, settling onto my knees.

Before Dawn could reply, another figure in a swimsuit moved quickly from the bushes, crouching low. It was Dawn's friend Dori.

"We swam over. Early this morning," Dori whispered, nervously pushing at her curly red hair. "We waited here. In the bushes."

"But it's not allowed," I said, unable to hide my confusion. "If you're caught—"

"We had to talk to you," Dawn interrupted, raising her head to peep over the top of the bushes, then quickly ducking back down.

"We decided to risk it," Dori added.

"What—what's wrong?" I stammered. A red-and-black insect crawled up my shoulder. I brushed it away.

"The girls' camp. It's a nightmare," Dori whispered.

"Everyone calls it Camp *Nightmare* instead of Camp Nightmoon," Dawn added. "Strange things have been happening."

"Huh?" I gaped at her. Not far from us in the water, I could hear the shouts and splashes of the swimming race beginning. "What kinds of strange things?"

"Scary things," Dori replied, her expression solemn.

"Girls have disappeared," Dawn told me. "Just vanished from sight."

"And no one seems to care," Dori added in a trembling whisper.

"I don't believe it!" I uttered. "The same thing has happened here. At the boys' camp." I swallowed hard. "Remember Mike?"

Both girls nodded.

"Mike disappeared," I told them. "They removed his stuff, and he just disappeared."

"It's unbelievable," Dori said. "Three girls have gone from our camp."

"They announced that one was attacked by a bear," Dawn whispered.

"What about the other two?" I asked.

"Just gone," Dawn replied, the words catching in her throat.

I could hear whistles blowing in the water. The race had ended. Another one was being organized.

The sun disappeared once again behind high white clouds. Shadows lengthened and grew darker.

I told them quickly about Roger and Jay and the attack at the Forbidden Cabin. They listened in open-mouthed silence. "Just like at our camp," Dawn said.

"We have to do something," Dori said heatedly.

"We have to get together. The boys and the girls," Dawn whispered, peering once again over the tops of the leaves. "We have to make a plan."

"You mean to escape?" I asked, not really understanding.

The two girls nodded. "We can't stay here," Dawn said grimly. "Every day another girl disappears. And the counsellors act as if nothing is happening."

"I think they *want* us to get killed or something," Dori added with emotion.

"Have you written to your parents?" I asked.

"We write every day," Dori replied. "But we haven't heard from them."

I suddenly realized that I hadn't received any post from my parents, either. They had both promised to write every day. But I had been at camp for nearly a week, and I hadn't received a single piece of post.

"Visitors Day is next week," I said. "Our parents will be here. We can tell them everything."

"It may be too late," Dawn said grimly.

"Everyone is so scared!" Dori declared. "I haven't slept for two nights. I hear these horrible screams outside every night."

Another whistle blew, closer to shore. I could hear the swimmers returning. Morning swim was over.

"I—I don't know what to say," I told them. "You've got to be careful. Don't get caught."

"We'll swim back to the girls' camp when everyone has left," Dawn said. "But we have to

90

meet again, Billy. We have to get more people together. You know. Maybe if we all get organized . . ." Her voice trailed off.

"There's something bad going on at this camp," Dori said with a shiver, narrowing her eyes. "Something evil."

"I—I know," I agreed. I could hear boys' voices now. Close by. Just on the other side of the leafy bushes. "I've got to go."

"We'll try to meet here again the day after tomorrow," Dawn whispered. "Be careful, Billy."

"*You* be careful," I whispered. "Don't get caught."

They slipped back, deeper in the bushes.

Crouching low, I made my way away from the shore. When I was past the clump of bushes, I stood up and began to run. I couldn't wait to tell Colin and Jay about what the girls had said.

I felt frightened and excited at the same time. I thought maybe it would make Jay feel a bit better to know that the same kinds of horrible things were happening across the river at the girls' camp.

Halfway to the bunks, I had an idea. I stopped and turned towards the lodge.

I suddenly remembered seeing a pay phone on the wall on the side of the building. Someone had told me that phone was the only one campers were allowed to use.

I'll call Mum and Dad, I decided.

Why hadn't I thought of it before?

I can phone my parents, I realized, and tell them everything. I could ask them to come and get me. And they could get Jay, Colin, Dawn, and Dori, too.

Behind me, I saw my group heading towards the scratchball field, their swimming towels slung over their shoulders. I wondered if anyone had noticed that I was missing.

Jay and Colin were missing, too, I told myself. Larry and the others probably think I'm with them.

I watched them trooping across the tall grass in twos and threes. Then I turned and started jogging up the hill towards the lodge.

The idea of calling home had cheered me up already.

I was so eager to hear my parents' voices, so eager to tell them the strange things that were happening here.

Would they believe me?

Of *course* they would. My parents always believed me. Because they trusted me.

As I ran up the hill, the dark pay phone came into view on the white lodge wall. I started to run at full speed. I wanted to *fly* to the phone.

I hope Mum and Dad are home, I thought.

They've *got* to be home.

I was panting loudly as I reached the wall. I

lowered my hands to my knees and crouched there for a moment, waiting to catch my breath.

Then I reached up to take the receiver down.

And gasped.

The pay phone was plastic. Just a stage prop. A fake.

It was a thin sheet of moulded plastic held to the wall by a nail, made to look just like a telephone.

It wasn't real. It was a fake.

They don't want us to phone home, I thought with a sudden chill.

My heart thudding, my head spinning in bitter disappointment, I turned away from the wall—and bumped right into Uncle Al.

"Billy—what are you doing up here?" Uncle Al asked. He was wearing baggy green camp shorts and a sleeveless white T-shirt that revealed his meaty pink arms. He carried a brown clipboard filled with papers. "Where are you supposed to be?"

"I . . . uh . . . wanted to make a phone call," I stammered, taking a step back. "I wanted to phone my parents."

He eyed me suspiciously and fingered his yellow moustache. "Really?"

"Yeah. Just to say hi," I told him. "But the phone—"

Uncle Al followed my gaze to the plastic phone. He chuckled. "Someone put that up as a joke," he said, grinning at me. "Did it fool you?"

"Yeah," I admitted, feeling my face grow hot. I raised my eyes to his. "Where is the real phone?"

His grin faded. His expression turned serious. "No phone," he replied sharply. "Campers aren't allowed to call out. It's a rule, Billy."

"Oh." I didn't know what to say.

"Are you really homesick?" Uncle Al asked softly.

I nodded.

"Well, go and write your mum and dad a long letter," he said. "It'll make you feel a lot better."

"Okay," I said. I didn't think it *would* make me feel better. But I wanted to get away from Uncle Al.

He raised his clipboard and gazed at it. "Where are you supposed to be now?" he asked.

"Scratchball, I think," I replied. "I didn't feel too well, you see. So I—"

"And when is your canoe trip?" he asked, not listening to me. He flipped through the sheets of paper on the clipboard, glancing over them quickly.

"Canoe trip?" I hadn't heard about any canoe trip.

"Tomorrow," he said, answering his own question. "Your group goes tomorrow. Are you excited?" He lowered his eyes to mine.

"I—I didn't really know about it," I confessed.

"Lots of fun!" he exclaimed enthusiastically. "The river doesn't look like much up here. But it gets pretty exciting a few kilometres down. You'll find yourself in some good rapids."

He squeezed my shoulder briefly. "You'll enjoy it," he said, grinning. "Everyone always enjoys the canoe ride."

"Great," I said. I tried to sound a little excited, but my voice came out flat and uncertain.

Uncle Al gave me a wave with his clipboard and headed around towards the front of the lodge, taking long strides. I stood watching him till he disappeared around the corner of the building. Then I made my way down the hill to the cabin.

I found Colin and Jay on the grass at the side of the cabin. Colin had his shirt off and was sprawled on his back, his hands behind his head. Jay sat cross-legged beside him, nervously pulling up long, slender strands of grass, then tossing them down.

"Come inside," I told them, glancing around to make sure no one else could hear.

They followed me into the cabin. I closed the door.

"What's up?" Colin asked, dropping onto a lower bunk. He picked up his red bandanna and twisted it in his hands.

I told them about Dawn and Dori and what they had reported about the girls' camp.

Colin and Jay both reacted with shock.

"They really swam over here and waited for you?" Jay asked.

I nodded. "They think we have to get organized or escape or something," I said.

"They could get into big trouble if they get caught," Jay said thoughtfully.

"We're all in big trouble," I told him. "We have to get *out*!"

"Visitors Day is next week," Colin muttered.

"I'm going to write to my parents right now," I said, pulling out the case from under my bunk, where I kept my paper and pens. "I'm going to tell them I *have* to come home on Visitors Day."

"I think I will, too," Jay said, tapping his fingers nervously against the bunk frame.

"Me, too," Colin agreed. "It's just too ... weird here!"

I pulled out a couple of sheets of paper and sat down on the bed to write. "Dawn and Dori were really scared," I told them.

"So am I," Jay admitted.

I started to write my letter. I wrote *Dear Mum and Dad, HELP!* then stopped. I raised my eyes across the cabin to Jay and Colin. "Do you two know about the canoe trip tomorrow?" I asked.

They stared back at me, their expressions surprised.

"Whoa!" Colin declared. "A five-kilometre hike this afternoon, and a canoe trip tomorrow?"

It was my turn to be surprised. "Hike? What hike?"

"Aren't you coming on it?" Jay asked.

"You know that really tall counsellor? Frank? The one who wears the yellow cap?" Colin asked. "He told Jay and me we're going on a five-kilometre hike after lunch."

"No one told me," I replied, chewing on the end of my pen.

"Maybe you're not in the hike group," Jay said.

"You'd better ask Frank at lunch," Colin suggested. "Maybe he couldn't find you. Maybe you're supposed to come, too."

I groaned. "Who wants to go on a five-kilometre hike in this heat?"

Colin and Jay both shrugged.

"Frank said we'd really like it," Colin told me, knotting and unknotting the red bandanna.

"I just want to get out of here," I said, returning to my letter.

I wrote quickly, intensely. I wanted to tell my parents all the frightening, strange things that had happened. I wanted to make them see why I couldn't stay at Camp Nightmoon.

I had written nearly a page and a half, and I was up to the part where Jay and Roger went out to explore the Forbidden Cabin, when Larry burst in. "You boys taking the day off?" he asked, his eyes going from one of us to the other. "You think this is a holiday or something?"

"Just messing about," Jay replied.

I folded up my letter and started to tuck it under my pillow. I didn't want Larry to see it. I realized I didn't trust Larry at all. I had no reason to.

"What are *you* doing, Billy?" he asked

suspiciously, his eyes stopping on the letter I was shoving under the pillow.

"Just writing home," I replied softly.

"You homesick or something?" he asked, a grin spreading across his face.

"Maybe," I muttered.

"Well, it's lunchtime, boys," he announced. "Let's go, okay?"

We all climbed out of our bunks.

"Jay and Colin are going on a hike with Frank this afternoon, I heard," Larry said. "Lucky boys." He turned and started out of the door.

"Larry!" I called to him. "Hey, Larry—what about me? Am I supposed to go on the hike, too?"

"Not today," he called back.

"But why not?" I said.

But Larry disappeared out of the door.

I turned back to my two cabin mates. "Lucky boys!" I teased them.

They both growled back at me in reply. Then we headed up the hill for lunch.

They served pizza for lunch, which is usually my favourite. But today, the pizza was cold and tasted like cardboard, and the cheese stuck to the roof of my mouth.

I wasn't really hungry.

I kept thinking about Dawn and Dori, how frightened they were, how desperate. I wondered when I'd see them again. I wondered if they would swim over and hide at the boys' camp again before Visitors Day.

After lunch, Frank came by our table to pick up Jay and Colin. I asked him if I was supposed to come, too.

"You weren't on the list, Billy," he said, scratching at a mosquito bite on his neck. "I can only take two at a time, you know? The trail gets a little dangerous."

"Dangerous?" Jay asked, climbing up from the table.

Frank grinned at him. "You're a big strong lad," he told Jay. "You'll do okay."

I watched Frank lead Colin and Jay out of the refectory. Our table was empty now, except for a couple of blond-haired boys I didn't know who were arm-wrestling down at the end near the wall.

I pushed my tray away and stood up. I wanted to go back to the cabin and finish the letter to my parents. But as I took a few steps towards the door, I felt a hand on my shoulder.

I turned to see Larry grinning down at me. "Tennis tournament," he said.

"Huh?" I reacted with surprise.

"Billy, you're representing Cabin 4 in the tennis tournament," Larry said. "Didn't you see the lineup? It was posted on the announcements board."

"But I'm a terrible tennis player!" I protested.

"We're counting on you," Larry replied. "Get a racquet and get your bod down to the courts!"

I spent the afternoon playing tennis. I beat a little kid in straight sets. I had the feeling he had never held a tennis racquet before. Then I lost a long, hard-fought match to one of the blond-haired boys who'd been arm-wrestling at lunch.

I was drowning in sweat, and every muscle in my body ached when the match was over. I headed to the riverbank for a refreshing swim.

Then I returned to the cabin, changed into jeans and a green-and-white Camp Nightmoon T-shirt, and finished my letter to my parents.

It was nearly dinnertime. Jay and Colin weren't back from their hike yet. I decided to go up to the lodge and post my letter. As I headed up the hill, I saw clusters of kids hurrying to their cabins to change for dinner. But no sign of my two cabin mates.

Holding the letter tightly, I headed round to the back of the lodge building where the camp office was located. The door was wide open, so I walked in. A young woman was usually behind the counter to answer questions and to take the letters to be posted.

"Anyone here?" I called, leaning over the counter and peering into the tiny back room, which was dark.

No reply.

101

"Hi. Anyone here?" I repeated, clutching the envelope.

No. The office was empty.

Disappointed, I started to leave. Then I glimpsed the large burlap bag on the floor just inside the tiny back room.

The mailbag!

I decided to put my letter in the bag with the others to be posted. I slipped around the counter and into the back room and crouched down to put my envelope into the bag.

To my surprise, the mailbag was stuffed full of letters. As I pulled the bag open and started to shove my letter inside, a bunch of letters fell out onto the floor.

I started to scoop them up when a letter caught my eye.

It was one of mine. Addressed to my parents.

One I had written yesterday.

"Weird," I muttered aloud.

Bending over the bag, I reached in and pulled out a big handful of letters. I sifted through them quickly. I found a letter Colin had written.

I pulled out another pile.

And my eyes fell upon two other letters I had written nearly a week ago when I'd first arrived at camp.

I stared at them, feeling a cold chill run down my back.

All of our letters, all of the letters we had

written since the first day of camp, were here. In this mailbag.

None of them had been posted.

We couldn't phone home.

And we couldn't *write* home.

Frantically, my hands trembling, I began shoving the envelopes back into the mailbag.

What is going on here? I wondered. *What is going on?*

By the time I got to the refectory, Uncle Al was finishing the evening announcements. I slid into my seat, hoping I hadn't missed anything important.

I expected to see Jay and Colin opposite my place at the table. But their places were empty.

That's strange, I thought, still shaken from my discovery about the mailbag. They should be back by now.

I wanted to tell them about the post. I wanted to share the news that our parents weren't getting any of the letters we wrote.

And we weren't getting any of theirs.

The camp had to be keeping our post from us, I suddenly realized.

Colin and Jay—where are you?

The fried chicken was greasy, and the potatoes were lumpy and tasted like paste. As I forced the food down, I kept turning to glance at the refectory door, expecting to see my two cabin mates.

But they didn't show up.

A heavy feeling of dread formed in my stomach. Through the refectory window, I could see that it was already dark outside.

Where could they be?

A five-kilometre hike and back shouldn't take this many hours.

I pulled myself up and made my way to the counsellors' table in the corner. Larry was having a loud argument about sport with two of the other counsellors. They were shouting and gesturing with their hands.

Frank's chair was empty.

"Larry, did Frank get back?" I interrupted their discussion.

Larry turned, a startled expression on his face. "Frank?" He motioned to the empty chair at the table. "Suppose not."

"He took Jay and Colin on the hike," I said. "Shouldn't they be back by now?"

Larry shrugged. "Beats me." He returned to his argument, leaving me standing there staring at Frank's empty chair.

After the trays had been cleared away, we pushed the tables and benches against the wall and had indoor relay races. Everyone seemed to be having a great time. The shouts and cheers echoed off the high-raftered ceiling.

I was too worried about Jay and Colin to enjoy the games.

Maybe they decided to camp out overnight, I told myself.

But I had seen them leave, and I knew they hadn't taken any tents or sleeping bags or other overnight supplies.

So where *were* they?

The games finished a little before lights out. As I followed the crowd to the door, Larry appeared beside me. "We're leaving early tomorrow morning," he said. "First thing."

"Huh?" I didn't understand what he meant.

"The canoe trip. I'm the canoe counsellor. I'll be taking you boys," he explained, seeing my confusion.

"Oh. Okay," I replied without enthusiasm. I was so worried about Jay and Colin, I'd nearly forgotten about the canoe trip.

"Straight after breakfast," Larry said. "Wear your swimming trunks. Bring a change of clothes. Meet me at the riverbank." He hurried back to help the other counsellors pull the tables into place.

"After breakfast," I muttered. I wondered if Jay and Colin were also coming on the canoe trip. I had forgotten to ask Larry.

I headed quickly down the dark hill. The dew had already fallen, and the tall grass was slippery and wet. Halfway down, I could see the dark outline of the Forbidden Cabin, hunched forward as if preparing to strike.

Forcing myself to look away, I jogged the rest of the way to Cabin 4.

To my surprise, I could see through the window that someone was moving around inside.

Colin and Jay are back! I thought.

Eagerly, I pushed open the door and burst inside. "Hey—where've you two been?" I cried.

I stopped short. And gasped.

Two strangers stared back at me.

One was sitting on the edge of Colin's top bunk, pulling off his trainers. The other was leaning over the chest of drawers, pulling a T-shirt from one of the drawers.

"Hi. You in here?" the boy at the chest of drawers stood up straight, his eyes studying me. He had very short black hair, and a gold stud in one ear.

I swallowed hard. "Am I in the wrong cabin? Is this Cabin 4?"

They both stared at me, confused.

I saw the other boy, the one in Colin's bunk, also had black hair, but his was long and straggly and fell over his forehead. "Yeah. This is Cabin 4," he said.

"We're new," the short-haired boy added. "I'm Tommy, and he's Chris. We just started today."

"Hi," I said uncertainly. "My name's Billy." My heart was pounding like a drum in my chest. "Where are Colin and Jay?"

107

"Who?" Chris asked. "They told us this cabin was mostly empty."

"Well, Colin and Jay—" I started.

"We've just arrived. We don't know anyone," Tommy interrupted. He pushed the drawer shut.

"But that's Jay's drawer," I said, bewildered, pointing. "What did you do with Jay's stuff?"

Tommy gazed back at me in surprise. "The drawer was empty," he replied.

"Almost all the drawers were empty," Chris added, tossing his trainers down to the floor. "Except for the bottom two drawers."

"That's my stuff," I said, my head spinning. "But Colin and Jay—their stuff was here," I insisted.

"The whole cabin was empty," Tommy said. "Maybe your friends were moved."

"Maybe," I said weakly. I sat down on the lower bunk beneath my bed. My legs felt shaky. A million thoughts were whirring through my mind, all of them frightening.

"This is weird," I said aloud.

"It's not a bad cabin," Chris said, pulling down his blanket and settling in. "Quite cosy."

"How long are you staying at camp?" Tommy asked, pulling on a baggy white T-shirt. "All summer?"

"No!" I exclaimed with a shudder. "I'm not staying!" I spluttered. "I mean—I mean . . . I'm leaving. On ... uh ... I'm leaving on Visitors Day next week."

Chris flashed Tommy a surprised glance. "Huh? When are you leaving?" he asked again.

"On Visitors Day," I repeated. "When my parents come up for Visitors Day."

"But didn't you hear Uncle Al's announcement before dinner?" Tommy asked, staring hard at me. "Visitors Day has been cancelled!"

I drifted in and out of a troubled sleep that night. Even with the blanket pulled up to my chin, I felt shivery and afraid.

It felt so weird to have two strange boys in the bunk, sleeping where Jay and Colin slept. I was worried about my missing friends.

What had happened to them? Why hadn't they come back?

As I tossed restlessly in the top bunk, I heard howls in the distance. Animal cries, probably coming from the Forbidden Cabin. Long, frightening howls carried by the wind into our open cabin window.

At one point, I thought I heard kids screaming. I sat up straight, suddenly alert, and listened.

Had I dreamed the frightful shrieks? I was so scared and confused, it was impossible to tell what was real and what was a nightmare.

It took hours to get back to sleep.

I awoke to a grey, overcast morning, the air heavy and cold. Pulling on swimming trunks and a T-shirt, I raced to the lodge to find Larry. I had to find out what had happened to Jay and Colin.

I searched everywhere for him without success. Larry wasn't at breakfast. None of the other counsellors admitted to knowing anything. Frank, the counsellor who had taken my two friends on the hike, was also missing.

I finally found Larry at the riverbank, preparing a long metal canoe for our river trip. "Larry—where are they?" I cried out breathlessly.

He gazed up at me, holding an armload of canoe paddles. His expression turned to bewilderment. "Huh? Chris and Tommy? They'll be here soon."

"No!" I cried, grabbing his arm. "Jay and Colin! Where are they? What happened to them, Larry? You've *got* to tell me!"

I gripped his arm tightly. I was gasping for breath. I could feel the blood pulsing at my temples. "You've got to tell me!" I repeated shrilly.

He pulled away from me and let the paddles fall beside the canoe. "I don't know anything about them," he replied quietly.

"But Larry!"

"Really, I don't," he insisted in the same quiet voice. His expression softened. He placed a hand on my trembling shoulder. "Tell you what, Billy," he said, staring hard into my eyes. "I'll ask Uncle Al about it after our trip, okay? I'll find out for you. When we get back."

I stared back at him, trying to decide if he was being honest.

I couldn't tell. His eyes were as calm and cold as marbles.

He leaned forward and pushed the canoe into the shallow river water. "Here. Take one of those life jackets," he said, pointing to a pile behind me. "Strap it on. Then get in."

I did as he instructed. I saw that I had no choice.

Chris and Tommy came running up to us a few seconds later. They obediently followed Larry's instructions and strapped on the life-jackets.

A few minutes later, the four of us were seated cross-legged inside the long, slender canoe, drifting slowly away from the shore.

The sky was still charcoal-grey, the sun hidden behind hovering, dark clouds. The canoe bumped over the choppy river waters. The current was stronger than I had realized. We began to pick up speed. The low trees and shrubs along the riverbank slid past rapidly.

Larry sat facing us in the front of the canoe.

He demonstrated how to paddle as the river carried us away.

He watched us carefully, a tight frown on his face, as the three of us struggled to pick up the rhythm he was showing us. Then, when we finally seemed to catch on, Larry grinned and carefully turned round, gripping the sides of the canoe as he shifted his position.

"The sun is trying to come out," he said, his voice muffled in the strong breeze over the rippling water.

I glanced up. The sky looked darker than before.

He stayed with his back to us, facing forward, allowing the three of us to do the paddling. I had never paddled a canoe before. It was harder than I'd imagined. But as I fell into the rhythm of it with Tommy and Chris, I began to enjoy it.

Dark water smacked against the prow of the canoe, sending up splashes of white froth. The current grew stronger, and we picked up speed. The air was still cold, but the steady work of rowing warmed me. After a while, I realized I was sweating.

We rowed past tangles of yellow and grey-trunked trees. The river suddenly divided in two, and we shifted our paddles to take the left branch. Larry began paddling again, working to keep us off the tall rocks that jutted between the river branches.

The canoe bobbed up and slapped down. Bobbed up and slapped down. Cold water poured over the sides.

The sky darkened even more. I wondered if it was about to storm.

As the river widened, the current grew rapid and strong. I realized we didn't really need to paddle. The river current was doing most of the work.

The river sloped down. Wide swirls of frothing white water made the canoe leap and bounce.

"Here come the rapids!" Larry shouted, cupping his hands around his mouth so we could hear him. "Hang on! It gets pretty choppy!"

I felt a tremor of fear as a wave of icy water splashed over me. The canoe rose up on a shelf of white water, then hit hard as it landed.

I could hear Tommy and Chris laughing excitedly behind me.

Another icy wave rolled over the canoe, startling me. I cried out and nearly let go of my paddle.

Tommy and Chris laughed again.

I took a deep breath and held on tightly to the paddle, struggling to keep up the rhythm.

"Hey, look!" Larry cried suddenly.

To my astonishment, he climbed to his feet. He leaned forward, pointing into the swirling, white water.

"Look at those fish!" he shouted.

As he leaned down, the canoe was jarred by a powerful rush of current. The canoe spun to the right.

I saw the startled look on Larry's face as he lost his balance. His arms shot forward, and he plunged headfirst into the tossing waters.

"Noooooo!" I screamed.

I glanced back at Tommy and Chris, who had stopped paddling and were staring into the swirling, dark waters, their expressions frozen in open-mouthed horror.

"Larry! Larry!" I was screaming the name over and over without realizing it.

The canoe continued to slide rapidly down the churning waters.

Larry didn't come up.

"Larry!"

Behind me, Tommy and Chris also called out his name, their voices shrill and frightened.

Where was he? Why didn't he swim to the surface?

The canoe was drifting farther and farther downriver.

"Larrrrrry!"

"We have to stop!" I screamed. "We have to slow down!"

"We can't!" Chris shouted back. "We don't know how!"

Still no sign of Larry. I realized he must be in trouble.

Without thinking, I tossed my paddle into the river, climbed to my feet, and plunged into the dark, swirling waters to save him.

I jumped without thinking and swallowed a mouthful of the brown water as I went down.

My heart thudded in my chest as I struggled frantically to the surface, spluttering and choking.

Gasping in a deep breath, I lowered my head and tried to swim against the current. My trainers felt as if they weighed a tonne.

I realized I should have pulled them off before I jumped.

The water heaved and tossed. I moved my arms in long, desperate strokes, pulling myself towards the spot where Larry had fallen in. Glancing back, I saw the canoe, a dark blur growing smaller and smaller.

"Wait!" I wanted to shout to Tommy and Chris. "Wait for me to get Larry!"

But I knew that they didn't know how to slow down the canoe. They were helpless as the current carried them away.

Where was Larry?

I sucked in another mouthful of air—and froze as I felt a sharp cramp in my right leg.

The pain shot up through my entire right side.

I slid under the water and waited for the pain to lessen.

The cramp seemed to tighten until I could barely move the leg. Water rushed over me. I struggled to pull myself up to the surface.

As I choked in more air, I swam rapidly and hard, pulling myself up, ignoring the sharp pain in my leg.

Hey!

What was that object floating just ahead of me? A piece of driftwood being carried by the current?

Brown water washed over me, blinding me, tossing me back. Spluttering, I pulled myself back up.

Water rolled down my face. I struggled to see.

Larry!

He came floating right up to me.

"Larry! Larry!" I managed to scream.

But he didn't answer me. I could see clearly now that he was floating face down.

The leg cramp miraculously vanished as I reached out with both arms and grabbed Larry's shoulders. I pulled his head up from the water, rolled him onto his back, and wrapped my arm around his neck. I was using the lifesaving technique my parents had taught me.

Turning downriver, I searched for the canoe. But the current had carried it out of sight.

I swallowed another mouthful of icy water. Choking, I held onto Larry. I kicked hard. My right leg still felt tight and weak, but at least the pain had gone. Kicking and pulling with my free hand, I dragged Larry towards the shore.

To my relief, the current helped. It seemed to pull in the same direction.

A few seconds later, I was close enough to shore to stand. Wearily, panting like a wild animal, I tottered to my feet and dragged Larry onto the wet mud of the shore.

Was he dead? Had he drowned before I'd reached him?

I stretched him out on his back and, still panting loudly, struggling to catch my breath, to stop my whole body from trembling, I leaned over him.

And he opened his eyes.

He stared up at me blankly, as if he didn't recognize me.

Finally, he whispered my name. "Billy," he choked out, "are we okay?"

Larry and I rested for a bit. Then we walked back to camp, following the river upstream.

We were soaked through and covered in mud,

but I didn't care. We were alive. We were okay. I had saved Larry's life.

We didn't talk much all the way back. It was taking every ounce of strength we had just to walk.

I asked Larry if he thought Tommy and Chris would be okay.

"Hope so," he muttered, breathing hard. "They'll probably ride to shore and walk back like us."

I took this opportunity to ask him again about Jay and Colin. I thought maybe Larry would tell me the truth since we were completely alone and since I had just saved his life.

But he insisted he didn't know anything about my two cabin mates. As we walked, he raised one hand and swore he didn't know anything at all.

"So many frightening things have happened," I muttered.

He nodded, keeping his eyes straight ahead. "It's been strange," he agreed.

I waited for him to say more. But he walked on in silence.

It took three hours to walk back. We hadn't travelled downriver as far as I had thought, but the muddy shore kept twisting and turning, making our journey longer.

As the camp came into view, my knees buckled and my legs nearly collapsed under me.

Breathing hard, drenched in perspiration, our

clothes still damp and mud-splattered, we trudged wearily onto the riverbank.

"Hey—!" a voice called from the swimming area. Uncle Al, dressed in a baggy, green tracksuit, came hurrying across the mud to us. "What happened?" he asked Larry.

"We had an accident!" I cried before Larry had a chance to reply.

"I fell in," Larry admitted, his face reddening beneath the splattered mud. "Billy jumped in and saved me. We walked back."

"But Tommy and Chris couldn't stop the canoe. They drifted away!" I cried.

"We both nearly drowned," Larry told the frowning camp director. "But, Billy—he saved my life."

"Can you send someone to find Tommy and Chris?" I asked, suddenly starting to shake all over, from exhaustion, I suppose.

"The two boys floated on downriver?" Uncle Al asked, staring hard at Larry, scratching the back of his fringe of yellow hair.

Larry nodded.

"We have to find them!" I insisted, trembling harder.

Uncle Al continued to glare at Larry. "What about my canoe?" he demanded angrily. "That's our best canoe! How am I supposed to replace it?"

Larry shrugged unhappily.

"We'll have to go and look for that canoe tomorrow," Uncle Al snapped.

He doesn't care about the two boys, I realized. *He doesn't care about them at all.*

"Go and get into dry clothes," Uncle Al instructed Larry and me. He stormed off towards the lodge, shaking his head.

I turned and started for the cabin, feeling chilled, my body still trembling. I could feel a strong wave of anger sweep over me.

I had just saved Larry's *life*, but Uncle Al didn't care about that.

And he didn't care that two campers were lost on the river.

He didn't care that two campers and a counsellor had never returned from their hike.

He didn't care that boys were attacked by *creatures!*

He didn't care that kids disappeared and were never mentioned again.

He didn't care about any of us.

He only cared about his canoe.

My anger quickly turned to fear.

Of course, I had no way of knowing that the *scariest* part of my summer was yet to come.

I was all alone in the cabin that night.

I pulled an extra blanket onto my bed and slid into a tight ball beneath the covers. I wondered if I'd be able to fall asleep. Or if my frightened, angry thoughts would keep me tossing and turning for another night.

But I was so weary and exhausted, even the eerie, mournful howls from the Forbidden Cabin couldn't keep me awake.

I fell into deep blackness and didn't wake up until I felt someone shaking my shoulders.

Startled alert, I sat up straight. "Larry!" I cried, my voice still clogged with sleep. "What's happening?"

I squinted across the room. Larry's bed was rumpled, the blanket balled up at the end. He had obviously come in late and slept in the bunk.

But Tommy's and Chris's beds were still untouched from the day before.

"Special hike," Larry said, walking over to his bunk. "Hurry. Get dressed."

"Huh?" I stretched and yawned. Outside the window, it was still grey. The sun hadn't come up. "What kind of hike?"

"Uncle Al has called a special hike," Larry replied, his back to me. He grabbed the sheet and started to make his bed.

With a groan, I lowered myself to the cabin floor. It felt cold beneath my bare feet. "Don't we get to rest? I mean, after what happened yesterday?" I glanced once again at Tommy's and Chris's unused beds.

"It's not just us," Larry replied, smoothing the sheet. "It's the whole camp. Everyone's going. Uncle Al is leading it."

I pulled on a pair of jeans, stumbling across the cabin with one leg in. A sudden feeling of dread fell over me. "It wasn't scheduled," I said darkly. "Where is Uncle Al taking us?"

Larry didn't reply.

"Where?" I repeated shrilly.

He pretended he didn't hear me.

"Tommy and Chris—they didn't come back?" I asked glumly, pulling on my trainers. Luckily, I had brought two pairs. My shoes from yesterday sat in the corner, still soaked through and mud-covered.

"They'll turn up," Larry replied finally. But he didn't sound as if he meant it.

124

I finished getting dressed, then ran up the hill to get breakfast. It was a warm, grey morning. It must have rained during the night. The tall grass glistened wetly.

Yawning and blinking against the harsh grey light, campers headed quietly up the hill. I saw that most of them had the same confused expression I had.

Why were we going on this unscheduled hike so early in the morning? How long was it going to be? Where were we going?

I hoped that Uncle Al or one of the other counsellors would explain everything to us at breakfast, but none of them appeared in the refectory.

We ate quietly, without the usual joking around.

I found myself thinking about the terrifying canoe trip yesterday. I could almost taste the brackish brown water again. I saw Larry floating towards me, face down, floating on the churning water like a clump of seaweed.

I pictured myself trying to get him, struggling to swim, struggling to go against the current, to keep afloat in the swirls of white water.

And I saw the blur of the canoe as the strong river current carried it out of sight.

Suddenly Dawn and Dori burst into my thoughts. I wondered if they were okay. I wondered if they were going to try and meet me again by the riverbank.

Breakfast was French toast with syrup. It was usually my favourite. But this morning, I just poked at it with my fork.

"Line up outside!" a counsellor cried from the doorway.

Chairs scraped loudly. We all obediently climbed to our feet and began making our way outside.

Where were they taking us?

Why doesn't anyone tell us what this is about?

The sky had brightened to pink, but the sun still hadn't risen over the horizon.

We formed a single line along the side wall of the lodge. I was near the end of the line towards the bottom of the hill.

Some kids were cracking jokes and playfully shoving each other. But most were standing quietly or leaning against the wall, waiting to see what was going to happen.

Once the line was formed, one of the counsellors walked the length of it, pointing his finger and moving his lips in concentration as he counted us. He counted us twice to make sure he had the right number.

Then Uncle Al appeared at the front of the line. He wore a brown-and-green camouflage outfit, the kind soldiers wear in films. He had on very black sunglasses, even though the sun wasn't up yet.

He didn't say a word. He signalled to Larry and another counsellor, who were both carrying very large, heavy-looking brown bags over their shoulders. Then Uncle Al strode quickly down the hill, his eyes hidden behind the dark glasses, his features set in a tight frown.

He stopped in front of the last camper. "This way!" he announced loudly, pointing towards the riverbank.

Those were his only words. "This way!"

And we began to follow, walking at a pretty fast pace. Our trainers slid against the wet grass. A few kids were giggling about something behind me.

To my surprise, I realized I was now nearly at the front of the line. I was close enough to call out to Uncle Al. So I did. "Where are we going?" I shouted.

He quickened his pace and didn't reply.

"Uncle Al—is this a long hike?" I called.

He pretended he hadn't heard.

I decided to give up.

He led us towards the riverbank, then turned right. Thick clumps of trees stood a short way up ahead where the river narrowed.

Glancing back to the end of the line, I saw Larry and the other counsellors, bags on their shoulders, hurrying to catch up with Uncle Al.

What is this about? I wondered.

And as I stared at the clumps of low, tangled

127

trees up ahead, a thought pushed its way into my head.

I can escape.

The thought was so frightening—but suddenly so real—it took a long time to form.

I can escape into these trees.

I can run away from Uncle Al and this frightening camp.

The idea was so exciting, I nearly stumbled over my own feet. I bumped into the kid ahead of me, a big bruiser of a boy called Tyler, and he turned and glared at me.

Whoa, I told myself, feeling my heart start to pound in my chest. Think about this. Think carefully. . . .

I kept my eyes locked on the woods. As we drew closer, I could see that the thick trees, so close together that their branches were all intertwined, seemed to stretch on forever.

They'd never find me in there, I told myself. It would be really easy to hide in those woods.

But then what?

I couldn't stay in the woods forever.

Then what?

Staring at the trees, I forced myself to concentrate, forced myself to think clearly.

I could follow the river. Yes. Stay on the shore. Follow the river. It was bound to come to a town eventually. It *had* to come to a town.

I'd walk to the first town. Then I'd call my parents.

I can do it, I thought, so excited I could barely stay in line.

I just have to run. Make a dash for it. When no one is looking. Into the woods. Deep into the woods.

We were at the edge of the trees now. The sun had pulled itself up, brightening the rose-coloured morning sky. We stood in the shadows of the trees.

I can do it, I told myself.

Soon.

My heart thudded loudly. I was sweating even though the air was still cool.

Calm down, Billy, I warned myself. *Just calm down.*

Wait your chance.

Wait till the time is right.

Then leave Camp Nightmare behind. Forever.

Standing in the shade, I studied the trees. I spotted a narrow path into the woods a few metres up ahead.

I tried to calculate how long it would take me to reach the path. Probably ten seconds at the most. And, then, in another five seconds, I could be into the protection of the trees.

I can do it, I thought.

I can be away in less than ten seconds.

I took a deep breath. I braced myself. I tensed my leg muscles, preparing to run.

Then I glanced to the front of the line.

To my horror, Uncle Al was staring directly at me. And he held a rifle in his hands.

I cried out when I saw the rifle in his hands.

Had he read my thoughts? Did he know I was about to make a run for it?

A cold chill slid down my back as I gaped at the rifle. As I raised my eyes to Uncle Al's face, I realized he wasn't looking at me.

He had turned his attention to the two counsellors. They had lowered the bags to the ground and were bending over them, trying to get them open.

"Why did we stop?" Tyler, the kid ahead of me, asked.

"Is the hike over?" another kid joked. A few kids laughed.

"Can we go back now?" said another kid.

I stood watching in disbelief as Larry and the other counsellor began unloading rifles from the two bags.

"Line up and get one," Uncle Al instructed us, tapping the handle of his own rifle against the ground. "One rifle per boy. Come on—hurry!"

No one moved. I think everyone thought Uncle Al was kidding or something.

"What's *wrong* with you boys? I said *hurry!*" he snapped angrily. He grabbed up an armload of rifles and began moving down the line, pushing one into each boy's hands.

He pushed a rifle against my chest so hard, I staggered back a few steps. I grabbed it by the barrel before it fell to the ground.

"What's going on?" Tyler asked me.

I shrugged, studying the rifle with horror. I'd never held any kind of real gun before. My parents were both opposed to firearms of all kinds.

A few minutes later, we were all lined up in the shadow of the trees, each holding a rifle. Uncle Al stood near the middle of the line and motioned us into a tight circle so we could hear him.

"What's going on? Is this target practice?" one boy asked.

Larry and the other counsellor sniggered at that. Uncle Al's features remained hard and serious.

"Listen up!" he barked. "No more jokes. This is serious business."

The circle of campers tightened round him. We grew silent. A bird squawked noisily in a nearby tree. Somehow it reminded me of my plan to escape.

Was I about to be really sorry that I hadn't made a run for it?

"Two girls escaped from the girls' camp last night," Uncle Al announced in a flat, business-like tone. "A blonde and a redhead."

Dawn and Dori! I exclaimed to myself. I bet it was them!

"I believe," Uncle Al continued, "that these are the same two girls who sneaked over to the boys' camp and hid near the riverbank a few days ago."

Yes! I thought happily. It *is* Dawn and Dori! They escaped!

I suddenly realized a broad smile had broken out on my face. I quickly forced it away before Uncle Al could see my happy reaction to the news.

"The two girls are in these woods, boys. They're nearby," Uncle Al continued. He raised his rifle. "Your guns are loaded. Aim carefully when you see them. They won't get away from us!"

"Huh?" I gasped in disbelief. "You mean we're supposed to *shoot* them?"

I glanced around the circle of campers. They all looked as dazed and confused as I did.

"Yeah. You're supposed to shoot them," Uncle Al replied coldly. "I *told* you—they're trying to escape."

"But we can't!" I cried.

"It's easy," Uncle Al said. He raised his rifle to his shoulder and pretended to fire it. "See? Nothing to it."

"But we can't kill people!" I insisted.

"Kill?" His expression changed behind the dark glasses. "I didn't say anything about killing, did I? These guns are loaded with tranquillizer darts. We just want to stop these girls—not hurt them."

Uncle Al took two steps towards me, the rifle still in his hands. He stood over me menacingly, lowering his face close to mine.

134

"You got a problem with that, Billy?" he demanded.

He was challenging me.

I saw the other boys back away.

The woods grew silent. Even the birds stopped squawking.

"You got a problem with that?" Uncle Al repeated, his face so close to mine, I could smell his sour breath.

Terrified, I took a step back, then another.

Why was he doing this to me? Why was he challenging me like this?

I took a deep breath and held it. Then I screamed as loudly as I could: "I—I won't do it!"

Without completely realizing what I was doing, I raised the rifle to my shoulder and aimed the barrel at Uncle Al's chest.

"You're gonna be sorry," Uncle Al growled in a low voice. He tore off the sunglasses and heaved them into the woods. Then he narrowed his eyes furiously at me. "Drop the rifle, Billy. I'm gonna make you sorry."

"No," I told him, standing my ground. "You're not. Camp is over. You're not going to do anything."

My legs were trembling so hard, I could barely stand.

But I wasn't going to go hunting Dawn and Dori. I wasn't going to do anything else Uncle Al said. Ever.

"Give me the rifle, Billy," he said in his low, menacing voice. He reached out a hand towards my gun. "Hand it over, boy."

"No!" I cried.

"Hand it over, now," he ordered, his eyes narrowed, burning into mine. "Now!"

"No!" I cried.

He blinked once. Twice.

Then he leapt at me.

I took a step back with the rifle aimed at Uncle Al—and pulled the trigger.

The rifle emitted a soft *pop*.

Uncle Al tossed his head back and laughed. He let his rifle drop to the ground at his feet.

"Hey—!" I cried out, confused. I kept the rifle aimed at his chest.

"Congratulations, Billy," Uncle Al said, grinning warmly at me. "You passed." He stepped forward and reached out his hand to shake mine.

The other campers dropped their rifles. Glancing at them, I saw that they were all grinning, too. Larry, also grinning, flashed me a thumbs-up sign.

"What's going on?" I demanded suspiciously. I slowly lowered the rifle.

Uncle Al grabbed my hand and squeezed it hard. "Congratulations, Billy. I *knew* you'd pass."

"Huh? I don't understand!" I screamed, totally frustrated.

But instead of explaining anything to me,

Uncle Al turned to the trees and shouted, "Okay, everyone! It's over! He passed! Come out and congratulate him!"

And as I stared in disbelief, my wide-open mouth hanging down around my knees, people began stepping out from behind the trees.

First came Dawn and Dori.

"You *were* hiding in the woods!" I cried.

They laughed in response. "Congratulations!" Dawn cried.

And then others came out, grinning and congratulating me. I screamed when I recognized Mike. He was okay!

Beside him were Jay and Roger!

Colin stepped out of the woods, followed by Tommy and Chris. All smiling and happy and okay.

"What—what's going *on* here?" I stammered. I was totally stunned. I felt dizzy.

I didn't get it. I really didn't get it.

And then my mum and dad stepped out from the trees. Mum rushed up and gave me a hug. Dad patted the top of my head. "I knew you'd pass, Billy," he said. I could see happy tears in his eyes.

Finally, I couldn't take it any more. I pushed Mum gently away. "Passed *what*?" I demanded. "What *is* this? What's going on?"

Uncle Al put his arm around my shoulders and guided me away from the group of campers.

Mum and Dad followed close behind.

"This isn't really a summer camp," Uncle Al explained, still grinning at me, his face bright pink. "It's a government-testing lab."

"Huh?" I swallowed hard.

"You know your parents are scientists, Billy," Uncle Al continued. "Well, they're about to leave on a very important expedition. And this time they wanted to take you along with them."

"How come you didn't tell me?" I asked my parents.

"We couldn't!" Mum exclaimed.

"According to government rules, Billy," Uncle Al continued, "children aren't allowed to go on official expeditions unless they pass certain tests. That's what you've been doing here. You've been taking tests."

"Tests to see what?" I demanded, still dazed.

"Well, we wanted to see if you could obey orders," Uncle Al explained. "You passed when you refused to go to the Forbidden Cabin." He held up two fingers. "Second, we had to test your bravery. You demonstrated that by rescuing Larry." He held up a third finger. "Third, we had to see if you knew when *not* to follow orders. You passed that test by refusing to hunt for Dawn and Dori."

"And everyone was in on it?" I asked. "All the campers? The counsellors? Everyone? They were all actors?"

Uncle Al nodded. "They all work here at the testing lab." His expression turned serious. "You see, Billy, your parents want to take you to a very dangerous place, perhaps the most dangerous place in the known universe. So we had to make sure you can handle it."

The most dangerous place in the universe?

"Where?" I asked my parents. "Where are you taking me?"

"It's a very strange planet called Earth," Dad replied, glancing at Mum. "It's very far from here. But it could be exciting. The inhabitants there are weird and unpredictable, and no one has ever studied them."

Laughing, I stepped between my mum and dad and put my arms around them. "Earth?! It sounds pretty weird. But it could *never* be as dangerous or exciting as Camp Nightmoon!" I explained.

"We'll see," Mum replied quietly. "We'll see."

Piano Lessons
Can Be Murder

I thought I was going to hate moving into a new house. But actually, I had fun.

I played a pretty mean joke on Mum and Dad.

While they were busy in the front room showing the removal men where to put stuff, I went exploring. I found a really great room to the side of the dining room.

It had big windows on two sides looking out onto the back garden. Sunlight poured in, making the room brighter and a lot more cheery than the rest of the old house.

The room was going to be our new family room. You know, with a TV and CD player, and maybe a ping-pong table and stuff. But right now it was completely empty.

Except for two grey balls of dust in one corner, which gave me an idea.

Chuckling to myself, I bent down and shaped the two dust balls with my hands. Then I began shouting in a really panicky voice: "Mice! Mice! Help! *Mice!*"

Mum and Dad came bursting into the room at the same time. Their mouths nearly dropped to the floor when they saw the two grey dust mice.

I kept screaming, "Mice! Mice!" Pretending I was scared of them. Trying hard to keep a straight face.

Mum just stood in the doorway, her mouth hanging open. I really thought she was going to drop her teeth!

Dad always panics more than Mum. He picked up a broom that was leaning against the wall, ran across the room, and began pounding the poor, defenceless dust mice with it.

By that time, I was laughing my head off.

Dad stared down at the glob of dust stuck to the end of the broom, and he finally caught on that it was a joke. His face got really red, and I thought his eyes were going to pop out from behind his glasses.

"Very funny, Jerome," Mum said calmly, rolling her eyes. Everyone calls me Jerry, but she calls me Jerome when she's upset with me. "Your father and I certainly appreciate your scaring us to death when we're both very nervous and overworked and trying to get moved into this house."

Mum is always really sarcastic like that. I

think I probably get my sense of humour from her.

Dad just scratched the bald spot on the back of his head. "They really looked like mice," he muttered. He wasn't angry. He's used to my jokes. They both are.

"Why can't you act your age?" Mum asked, shaking her head.

"I am!" I insisted. I mean, I'm twelve. So I *was* acting my age. If you can't play jokes on your parents and try to have a little fun at twelve, when *can* you?

"Don't be such a clever-dick," Dad said, giving me his stern look. "There's a lot of work to be done around here, you know, Jerry. You could help out."

He shoved the broom towards me.

I raised both hands as if shielding myself from danger, and backed away. "Dad, you *know* I'm allergic!" I cried.

"Allergic to dust?" he asked.

"No. Allergic to work!"

I expected them to laugh, but they just stormed out of the room, muttering to themselves. "You can at least look after Bonkers," Mum called back to me. "Keep her out of the removal men's way."

"Yeah. Sure," I called back. Bonkers is our cat, and there's *no way* I can keep Bonkers from doing anything!

Let me say straight away that Bonkers is *not* my favourite member of our family. In fact, I keep as far away from Bonkers as I can.

No one ever explained to the stupid cat that she's supposed to be a pet. Instead, I think Bonkers believes she's a wild, man-eating tiger. Or maybe a vampire bat.

Her favourite trick is to climb up on the back of a chair or a high shelf—and then leap with her claws out onto your shoulders. I can't tell you how many good T-shirts have been ripped to shreds by this trick of hers. Or how much blood I've lost.

The cat isn't nasty—just plain vicious.

She's all black except for a white circle over her forehead and one eye. Mum and Dad think she's just wonderful. They're always picking her up, and petting her, and telling her how adorable she is. Bonkers usually scratches them and makes them bleed. But they never learn.

When we moved to this new house, I was hoping maybe Bonkers would get left behind. But, no way. Mum made sure that Bonkers was in the car first, right next to me.

And of course the stupid cat threw up in the back seat.

Whoever heard of a cat who gets carsick? She did it deliberately because she's horrible and vicious.

Anyway, I ignored Mum's request to keep an eye on her. In fact, I crept into the kitchen and opened the back door, hoping maybe Bonkers would run away and get lost.

Then I continued my exploring.

Our other house was tiny, but new. This house was old. The floorboards creaked. The windows rattled. The house seemed to groan when you walked through it.

But it was really big. I discovered all kinds of little rooms and deep cupboards. One upstairs cupboard was as big as my old bedroom!

My new bedroom was at the end of the passage on the first floor. There were three other rooms and a bathroom up there. I wondered what Mum and Dad planned to do with all those rooms.

I decided to suggest that one of them be made into a Nintendo room. We could put a wide-screen TV in there to play the games on. It would be really great.

As I made plans for my new video game room, I started to feel a little cheered up. I mean, it isn't easy to move to a new house in a new town.

I'm not the kind of kid who cries much. But I have to admit that I felt like crying a *lot* when we moved away from Cedarville. Especially when I had to say goodbye to my friends.

Especially Sean. Sean is a great kid. Mum and Dad don't like him very much because he's kind of noisy and he likes to burp really loud. But Sean is my best friend.

I mean he *was* my best friend.

I don't have any friends here in New Goshen.

Mum said Sean could come and stay with us for a few weeks this summer. That was really nice of her, especially since she hates his burping so much.

But it didn't really cheer me up.

Exploring the new house was making me feel a little better. The room next to mine can be a gym, I decided. We'll get all those great-looking exercise machines they show on TV.

The removal men were hauling stuff into my room, so I couldn't go in there. I pulled open a door to what I thought was a cupboard. But to my surprise, I saw a narrow, wooden staircase. I supposed it led up to an attic.

An attic!

I'd never had an attic before. I bet it's filled with all kinds of great old stuff, I thought excitedly. Maybe the people who used to live here left their old comics collection up there—and it's worth millions!

I was halfway up the stairs when I heard Dad's voice behind me. "Jerry, where are you going?"

"Up," I replied. That was pretty obvious.

"You really shouldn't go up there by yourself," he warned.

"Why not? Are there ghosts up there or something?" I asked.

I could hear his heavy footsteps on the wooden stairs. He followed me up. "Hot up here," he muttered, adjusting his glasses on his nose. "It's so stuffy."

He tugged on a chain suspended from the ceiling, and an overhead light came on, casting pale yellow light down on us.

I glanced quickly around. It was all one room, long and low, the ceiling slanting down on both sides under the roof. I'm not very tall, but I reached up and touched the ceiling.

There were tiny, round windows at both ends. But they were covered with dust and didn't let in much light.

"It's empty," I muttered, very disappointed.

"We can store a lot of junk up here," Dad said, looking around.

"Hey—what's that?" I spotted something against the far wall and began walking quickly towards it. The floorboards squeaked and creaked under my trainers.

I saw a grey, quilted cover over something large. Maybe it's some kind of treasure chest, I thought.

No one could ever accuse me of not having a good imagination.

Dad was right behind me as I grabbed the heavy cover with both hands and pulled it away.

And stared at a shiny, black piano.

"Wow," Dad murmured, scratching his bald spot, staring at the piano with surprise. "Wow. Wow. Why did they leave *this* behind?"

I shrugged. "It looks like new," I said. I hit some keys with one finger. "Sounds good."

Dad hit some keys, too. "It's a really good piano," he said, rubbing his hand lightly over the keyboard. "I wonder what it's doing hidden up here in the attic like this. . ."

"It's a mystery," I agreed.

I had no idea how big a mystery it really was.

I couldn't get to sleep that night. I mean, there was no way.

I was in my good old bed from our old house. But it was facing the wrong direction. And it was against a different wall. And the light from the neighbour's back porch was shining through the window. The window rattled from the wind. And all these creepy shadows were moving back and forth across the ceiling.

I'm *never* going to be able to sleep in this new room, I realized.

It's too different. Too creepy. Too big.

I'm going to be awake for the rest of my life!

I just lay there, eyes wide open, staring up at the weird shadows.

I had just started to relax and drift off to sleep when I heard the music.

Piano music.

At first, I thought it was coming from outside. But I quickly realized it was coming from up above me. From the attic!

I sat straight up and listened. Yes. Some kind of classical music. Right over my head.

I kicked off the covers and lowered my feet to the floor.

Who could be up in the attic playing the piano in the middle of the night? I wondered. It couldn't be Dad. He can't play a note. And the only thing Mum can play is "Chopsticks", and not very well.

Maybe it's Bonkers, I told myself.

I stood up and listened. The music continued. Very softly. But I could hear it clearly. Every note.

I started to make my way to the door and stubbed my toe against a box that hadn't been unpacked. "Ow!" I cried out, grabbing my foot and hopping around until the pain faded.

Mum and Dad couldn't hear me, I knew. Their bedroom was downstairs.

I held my breath and listened. I could still hear the piano music above my head.

Walking slowly, carefully, I stepped out of my room and into the passage. The floorboards creaked under my bare feet. The floor was cold.

I pulled open the attic door and leaned into the darkness.

The music floated down. It was sad music, very slow, very soft.

"Who—who's up there?" I stammered.

The sad music continued, floating down the dark, narrow stairway to me.

"Who's up there?" I repeated, my voice shaking just a little.

Again, no reply.

I leaned into the darkness, peering up towards the attic. "Mum, is that you? Dad?"

No reply. The melody was so sad, so slow.

Before I even realized what I was doing, I was climbing the stairs. They groaned loudly under my bare feet.

The air grew hot and stuffy as I reached the top of the stairs and stepped into the dark attic.

The piano music surrounded me now. The notes seemed to be coming from all directions at once.

"Who is it?" I demanded in a shrill, high-pitched voice. I suppose I was a little scared. "Who's up here?"

Something brushed against my face, and I nearly jumped out of my skin.

It took me a long, shuddering moment to realize it was the light chain.

I pulled it. Pale yellow light spread out over the long, narrow room.

The music stopped.

"Who's up here?" I called, squinting towards the piano against the far wall.

No one.

No one there. No one sitting at the piano.

Silence.

Except for the floorboards creaking under my feet as I walked over to the piano. I stared at it, stared at the keys.

I don't know what I expected to see. I mean, *someone* was playing the piano. *Someone* played it until the exact second the light went on. Where did they go?

I ducked down and searched under the piano.

I know it was stupid, but I wasn't thinking clearly. My heart was pounding really hard, and all kinds of crazy thoughts were spinning through my brain.

I leaned over the piano and examined the keyboard. I thought maybe this was one of those old-fashioned pianos that played by itself. A player piano. You know, like you sometimes see in cartoons.

But it looked like an ordinary piano. I didn't see anything special about it.

I sat down on the bench.

And jumped up.

The piano bench was warm! As if someone had just been sitting on it!

"Who?" I cried aloud, staring at the shiny, black bench.

I reached down and felt it. It was definitely warm.

But I reminded myself that the whole attic was really warm, much warmer than the rest of the house. The heat seemed to float up here and stay.

I sat back down and waited for my racing heart to return to normal.

What's going on here? I asked myself, turning to stare at the piano. The black wood was polished so well, I could see the reflection of my face staring back at me.

My reflection looked pretty scared.

I lowered my eyes to the keyboard and then hit a few soft notes.

Someone had been playing this piano a few moments ago, I knew.

But how could they have vanished into thin air without me seeing them?

I plunked another note, then another. The sound echoed through the long, empty room.

Then I heard a loud creak. From the bottom of the stairs.

I froze, my hand still on the piano keys.

Another creak. A footstep.

I stood up, surprised to find my legs all trembly.

I listened. I listened so hard, I could hear the air move.

Another footstep. Louder. Closer.

Someone was on the stairs. Someone was climbing to the attic.

Someone was coming for me.

Creak. Creak.

The stairs gave way beneath heavy footsteps.

My breath caught in my throat. I felt as if I would suffocate.

Frozen in front of the piano, I searched for a place to hide. But of course there wasn't any.

Creak. Creak.

And then, as I stared in terror, a head poked up above the staircase.

"Dad!" I cried.

"Jerry, what on earth are you doing up here?" He stepped into the pale yellow light. His thinning brown hair was standing up all over his head. His pyjama bottoms were twisted. One leg had rolled up to the knee. He squinted at me. He didn't have his glasses on.

"Dad—I—I thought—" I spluttered. I knew I sounded like a complete jerk. But give me a break—I was *scared!*

"Do you know what time it is?" Dad demanded angrily. He glanced down at his wrist, but he wasn't wearing his watch. "It's the middle of the night, Jerry!"

"I—I know, Dad," I said, starting to feel a little better. I walked over to him. "I heard piano music, you see. And so I thought—"

"You *what?*" His dark eyes grew wide. His mouth dropped open. "You heard *what?*"

"Piano music," I repeated. "Up here. So I came upstairs to check it out, and—"

"Jerry!" Dad exploded. His face got really red. "It's too late for your silly jokes!"

"But, Dad—" I started to protest.

"Your mother and I killed ourselves unpacking and moving furniture all day," Dad said, sighing wearily. "We're both very exhausted, Jerry. I shouldn't have to tell you that I'm in no mood for jokes. 1 have to go to work tomorrow morning. I need some sleep."

"Sorry, Dad," I said quietly. I could see there was no way I was going to get him to believe me about the piano music.

"I know you're excited about being in a new house," Dad said, putting a hand on the shoulder of my pyjama top. "But, come on. Back to your room. You need your sleep, too."

I glanced back at the piano. It glimmered darkly in the pale yellow light. As if it were breathing. As if it were alive.

I pictured it rumbling towards me, chasing me to the stairs.

Crazy, weird thoughts. I suppose I was more tired than I thought!

"Would you like to learn to play it?" Dad asked suddenly.

"Huh?" His question caught me by surprise.

"Would you like to have piano lessons? We could have the piano brought downstairs. There's room for it in the family room."

"Well...maybe," I replied. "Yeah. That might be cool."

He took his hand from my shoulder. Then he straightened his pyjama bottoms and started downstairs. "I'll discuss it with your mother," he said. "I'm sure she'll be pleased. She always wanted someone to be musical in the family. Pull the light chain, okay?"

Obediently, I reached up and clicked off the light. The sudden darkness was so black, it startled me. I stayed close behind my dad as we made our way down the creaking stairs.

Back in my bed, I pulled the covers up to my chin. It was pretty cold in my room. Outside, the winter wind gusted hard. The bedroom window rattled and shook, as if it were shivering.

Piano lessons might be fun, I thought. If they let me learn to play rock music, not that drippy, boring classical stuff.

After a few lessons, maybe I could get a synthesizer. Get two or three different keyboards. Hook them up to a computer.

Then I could do some composing. Maybe get a group together.

Yeah. It could be really excellent.

I closed my eyes.

The window rattled again. The old house seemed to groan.

I'll get used to these noises, I told myself. I'll get used to this old house. After a few nights, I won't even hear the noises.

I had just about drifted off to sleep when I heard the soft, sad piano music begin again.

Monday morning I woke up very early. My cat clock with the moving tail and eyes wasn't unpacked yet. But I could tell it was early by the pale grey light coming through my bedroom window.

I got dressed quickly, pulling on a clean pair of faded jeans and a dark green pullover shirt that wasn't too wrinkled. It was my first day at my new school, so I was pretty excited.

I spent more time on my hair than I usually do. My hair is brown and thick and wiry, and it takes me a long time to slick it down and make it lie flat the way I like it.

When I finally got it right, I made my way down the hall to the front stairs. The house was still silent and dark.

I stopped outside the attic door. It was wide open.

Hadn't I closed it when I'd come downstairs with my dad?

Yes. I remembered shutting it tight. And now, here it was, wide open.

I felt a cold chill on the back of my neck. I closed the door, listening for the click.

Jerry, take it easy, I warned myself. Maybe the latch is loose. Maybe the attic door always swings open. It's an old house, remember?

I'd been thinking about the piano music. Maybe it was the wind blowing through the piano strings, I told myself.

Maybe there was a hole or something in the attic window. And the wind blew in and made it sound as if the piano was playing.

I wanted to believe it had been the wind that made that slow, sad music. I wanted to believe it, so I did.

I checked the attic door one more time, making sure it was latched, then headed down to the kitchen.

Mum and Dad were still in their room. I could hear them getting dressed.

The kitchen was dark and a little cold. I wanted to turn up the boiler, but I didn't know where the thermostat was.

Not all of our kitchen stuff had been unpacked. Boxes were still stacked against the wall, filled with glasses and plates and stuff.

I heard someone coming down the hall.

A big, empty packing case beside the fridge gave me an idea. Sniggering to myself, I jumped inside it and pulled the lid over me.

I held my breath and waited.

Footsteps in the kitchen. I couldn't tell if it was Mum or Dad.

My heart was pounding. I continued to hold my breath. If I didn't, I knew I would burst out laughing.

The footsteps went right past my packing case to the sink. I heard water running. Whoever it was had filled the kettle.

Footsteps to the cooker.

I couldn't wait any more.

"*SURPRISE!*" I screamed and jumped to my feet in the packing case.

Dad let out a startled shriek and dropped the kettle. It landed on his foot with a *thud*, then tilted onto its side on the floor.

Water puddled around Dad's feet. The kettle rolled towards the cooker. Dad was howling and holding his injured foot and hopping up and down.

I was laughing like a maniac! You should've seen the look on Dad's face when I jumped up from the case. I really thought he was going to drop his teeth!

Mum came bursting into the room, still buttoning her sleeve cuffs. "What's going on in here?" she cried.

"Just Jerry and his stupid jokes," Dad grumbled.

163

"Jerome!" Mum shouted, seeing all the spilled water on the lino. "Give us a break."

"Just trying to help wake you up," I said, grinning. They complain a lot, but they're used to my twisted sense of humour.

I heard the piano music again that night.

It was definitely not the wind. I recognized the same sad melody.

I listened for a few moments. It came from right above my room.

Who's up there? Who can be playing? I asked myself.

I started to climb out of bed and investigate. But it was cold in my room, and I was really tired from my first day at the new school.

So I pulled the covers over my head to drown out the piano music, and quickly fell asleep.

"Did you hear the piano music last night?" I asked my mum.

"Eat your cornflakes," she replied. She tightened the belt of her bathrobe and leaned towards me over the kitchen table.

"How come I have to have cornflakes?" I grumbled, mushing the spoon around in the bowl.

"You know the rules," she said, frowning. "Junk cereal only at weekends."

"Stupid rule," I muttered. "I think cornflakes is a junk cereal."

"Don't give me a hard time," Mum complained, rubbing her temples. "I have a headache this morning."

"From the piano playing last night?" I asked.

"What piano playing?" she demanded irritably. "Why do you keep talking about piano playing?"

"Didn't you hear it? The piano in the attic? Someone was playing it last night."

She jumped to her feet. "Oh, Jerry, please. No jokes this morning, okay? I told you I have a headache."

"Did I hear you talking about the piano?" Dad came into the kitchen, carrying the morning newspaper. "The men are coming this afternoon to carry it down to the family room." He smiled at me. "Limber up those fingers, Jerry."

Mum had walked over to the worktop to pour herself a cup of coffee. "Are you really interested in this piano?" she demanded, eyeing me sceptically. "Are you really going to practise and work at it?"

"Of course," I replied. "Maybe."

The two piano movers were there when I got home from school. They weren't very big, but they were strong.

I went up to the attic and watched them while Mum pulled packing cases out of the family room to make a place for it.

The two men used ropes and a special kind of dolly. They tilted the piano onto its side, then hoisted it onto the dolly.

Lowering it down the narrow staircase was really hard. It bumped against the wall several times, even though they moved slowly and carefully.

Both movers were really red-faced and sweaty by the time they got the piano downstairs. I followed them as they rolled it across the living room, then through the dining room.

Mum came out of the kitchen, her hands jammed into her jeans pockets, and watched from the doorway as they rolled the dolly with the piano into the family room.

The men strained to tilt it right side up. The black, polished wood really glowed in the bright afternoon sunlight through the family room windows.

Then, as they started to lower the piano to the floor, Mum opened her mouth and started to scream.

"The cat! The cat!" Mum shrieked, her face all twisted in alarm.

Sure enough, Bonkers was standing right in the spot where they were lowering the piano.

The piano thudded heavily to the floor. Bonkers ran out from under it just in time.

Too bad! I thought, shaking my head. That dumb cat almost got what it deserved.

The men were apologizing as they tried to catch their breath, mopping their foreheads with their handkerchiefs.

Mum ran to Bonkers and picked her up. "My poor little kitty."

Of course Bonkers swiped at Mum's arm, her claws tearing out several threads in the sweater sleeve. Mum dropped her to the floor, and the creature slithered quickly out of the room.

"She's a little nervous being in a new house," Mum told the two workers.

"She *always* acts like that," I told them.

A few minutes later, the men had gone. Mum was in her room, trying to mend her sweater. And I was alone in the family room with my piano.

I sat on the bench and slid back and forth on it. The bench was polished and smooth. It was really slippery.

I planned a really funny comedy act where I sit down to play the piano for Mum and Dad, only the bench is so slippery, I keep sliding right onto the floor.

I practised sliding and falling for a while. I was having fun.

Falling is one of my hobbies. It isn't as easy as it looks.

After a while, I got tired of falling. I just sat on the bench and stared at the keys. I tried picking out a tune, hitting notes until I found the right ones.

I started to get excited about learning to play the piano.

I imagined it was going to be fun.

I was wrong. Very wrong.

On Saturday afternoon, I stood staring out of the living room window. It was a blustery, grey day. It looked as if it was about to snow.

I saw the piano teacher walking up the drive. He was right on time. Two o'clock.

Pressing my face against the window, I could see that he was quite a big man. He wore a long, puffy red coat and he had bushy white hair. From this distance, he sort of looked like Santa Claus.

He walked very stiffly, as if his knees weren't good. Arthritis or something, I suppose.

Dad had found his name in a tiny ad in the back of the New Goshen newspaper. He showed it to me. It said:

THE SHREEK SCHOOL
New Method Piano Training

Since it was the only ad in the paper for a piano teacher, Dad phoned the number.

And now, Mum and Dad were greeting the teacher at the door and taking his heavy red coat. "Jerry, this is Dr Shreek," Dad said, motioning for me to leave my place by the window.

Dr Shreek smiled at me. "Hello, Jerry."

He really did look like Santa Claus, except he had a white moustache and no beard. He had round, red cheeks and a friendly smile, and his blue eyes sort of twinkled as he greeted me.

He wore a white shirt that was coming untucked around his big belly, and baggy, grey trousers.

I stepped forward and shook hands with him. His hand was red and kind of spongy. "Nice to meet you, Dr Shreek," I said politely.

Mum and Dad grinned at each other. They could never believe it when I was polite!

Dr Shreek put his spongy hand on my shoulder. "I know I have a funny name," he said, chuckling. "I probably should change it. But, you have to admit, it's a real attention-getter!"

We all laughed.

Dr Shreek's expression turned serious. "Have you ever played an instrument before, Jerry?"

I thought hard. "Well, I had a kazoo once!"

Everyone laughed again.

"The piano is a little more difficult than the kazoo," Dr Shreek said, still chuckling. "Let me see your piano."

I led him through the dining room and into the family room. He walked stiffly, but it didn't seem to slow him down.

Mum and Dad excused themselves and disappeared upstairs to do more unpacking.

Dr Shreek studied the piano keys. Then he lifted the back and examined the strings with his eyes. "Very fine instrument," he murmured. "Very fine."

"We found it here," I told him.

His mouth opened in a little O of surprise. "You found it!"

"In the attic. Someone just left it up there," I said.

"How strange," he replied, rubbing his pudgy chin. He straightened his white moustache as he stared at the keys. "Don't you wonder who played this piano before you?" he asked softly. "Don't you wonder whose fingers touched these keys?"

"Well . . ." I really didn't know what to say.

"What a mystery," he said in a whisper. Then he motioned for me to take a seat on the piano bench.

I was tempted to do my comedy act and slide right off onto the floor. But I decided I'd save it for when I knew him better.

He seemed like a nice, jolly kind of man. But I didn't want him to think I wasn't serious about learning to play.

He dropped down beside me on the bench. He was so wide, there was barely room for the two of us.

"Will you be giving me lessons here at home every week?" I asked, scooting over as far as I could to make room.

"I'll give you lessons at home at first," he replied, his blue eyes twinkling at me. "Then, if you show promise, Jerry, you can come to my school."

I started to say something, but he grabbed my hands.

"Let me take a look," he said, raising my hands close to his face. He turned them over and studied both sides. Then he carefully examined my fingers.

"What beautiful hands!" he exclaimed breathlessly. "Excellent hands!"

I stared down at my hands. They didn't look like anything special to me. Just normal hands.

"Excellent hands," Dr Shreek repeated. He placed them carefully on the piano keys. He showed me what each note was, starting with C, and he had me play each one with the correct finger.

"Next week we will start," he told me, climbing up from the piano bench. "I just wanted to meet you today."

He searched through a small bag he had leaned against the wall. He pulled out a workbook and handed it to me. It was called *Beginning to Play: A Hands-On Approach.*

"Look this over, Jerry. Try to learn the notes on pages two and three." He made his way over to his coat, which Dad had draped over the back of the sofa.

"See you next Saturday," I said. I felt a little disappointed that the lesson had been so short. I thought I'd be playing some great rock riffs by now.

He pulled on his coat, then came back to where I was sitting. "I think you will be an excellent pupil, Jerry," he said, smiling.

I muttered thanks. I was surprised to see that his eyes had settled on my hands. "Excellent. Excellent," he whispered.

I felt a sudden chill.

I think it was the hungry expression on his face.

What's so special about my hands? I wondered. *Why does he like them so much?*

It was weird. Definitely weird.

But of course I didn't know *how* weird . . .

CDEFGABC.

I practised the notes on pages two and three of the piano workbook. The book showed which finger to use and everything.

This is easy, I thought.

So when can I start playing some rock and roll?

I was still picking out notes when Mum surfaced from the basement and poked her head into the family room. Her hair had come loose from the bandanna she had tied around her head, and she had dirty smudges on her forehead.

"Has Dr Shreek left already?" she asked, surprised.

"Yeah. He said he just wanted to meet me," I told her. "He's coming back next Saturday. He said I had excellent hands."

"Have you?" She brushed the hair out of her eyes. "Well, maybe you can take those excellent

174

hands down to the basement and use them to help us unpack some boxes."

"Oh, no!" I cried, and I slid off the piano bench and fell to the floor.

She didn't laugh.

That night, I heard piano music.

I sat straight up in bed and listened. The music floated up from downstairs.

I climbed out of bed. The floorboards were cold under my bare feet. I was supposed to have a carpet, but Dad hadn't had time to put it down yet.

The house was silent. Through my bedroom window, I could see a gentle snow coming down, tiny, fine flakes, grey against the black sky.

"Someone is playing the piano," I said aloud, startled by the huskiness of my sleep-filled voice.

"Someone is downstairs playing my piano."

Mum and Dad must hear it, I thought. Their room is at the far end of the house. But they are downstairs. They must hear it.

I crept to my bedroom door.

The same slow, sad melody. I had been humming it just before dinner. Mum had asked me where I'd heard it, and I couldn't remember.

I leaned against the doorframe, my heart pounding, and listened. The music drifted up so clearly, I could hear each note.

Who is playing?

Who?

I had to find out. Trailing my hand along the wall, I hurried through the dark passage. There was a night-light by the stairway, but I was always forgetting to turn it on.

I made my way to the stairs. Then, gripping the wooden banister tightly, I crept down, one step at a time, trying to be silent.

Trying not to scare the piano player away.

The wooden stairs creaked quietly under my weight. But the music continued. Soft and sad, almost mournful.

Tiptoeing and holding my breath, I crossed the living room. A streetlight cast a wash of pale yellow across the floor. Through the large front window, I could see the tiny snowflakes drifting down.

I nearly tripped over an unpacked case of vases left next to the coffee table. But I grabbed the back of the sofa and kept myself from falling.

The music stopped. Then started again.

I leaned against the sofa, waiting for my heart to stop pounding so hard.

Where are Mum and Dad? I wondered, staring towards the back hallway where their room was.

Can't they hear the piano, too? Aren't they curious? Don't they wonder who is in the family room in the middle of the night, playing such a sad song?

I took a deep breath and pushed myself away from the sofa. Slowly, silently, I made my way through the dining room.

It was darker back there. No light from the street. I moved carefully, aware of all the chairs and table legs that could trip me up.

The door to the family room stood just a few feet ahead of me. The music grew louder.

I took a step. Then another.

I moved into the open doorway.

Who is it? Who is it?

I peered into the darkness.

But before I could see anything, someone uttered a horrifying shriek behind me—and shoved me hard, pushing me down to the floor.

I hit the floor hard on my knees and elbows.

Another loud shriek—right in my ears.

My shoulders throbbed with pain.

The light came on.

"Bonkers!" I roared.

The cat leapt off my shoulders and scurried out of the room.

"Jerry—what are you doing? What's going on?" Mum demanded angrily as she ran into the room.

"What's all the racket?" Dad was right behind her, squinting hard without his glasses.

"Bonkers jumped on me!" I screamed, still on the floor. "Ow. My shoulder. That stupid cat!"

"But, Jerry—" Mum started. She bent to help pull me up.

"That stupid cat!" I fumed. "She jumped down from that shelf. She scared me to death. And look—look at my pyjama top!"

178

The cat's claws had ripped right through the shoulder.

"Are you cut? Are you bleeding?" Mum asked, pulling the shirt collar down to examine my shoulder.

"We really have to do something about that cat," Dad muttered. "Jerry is right. She's a menace."

Mum immediately jumped to Bonkers' defence. "She was just frightened, that's all. She probably thought Jerry was a burglar."

"A burglar?" I shrieked in a voice so high, only dogs could hear me. "How could she think I was a burglar? Aren't cats supposed to see in the dark?"

"Well, what were you doing down here, Jerry?" Mum asked, straightening my pyjama top collar. She patted my shoulder. As if that would help.

"Yeah. Why were you skulking around down here?" Dad demanded, squinting hard at me. He could barely see a thing without his glasses.

"I wasn't skulking around," I replied angrily. "I heard piano music and—"

"You *what*?" Mum interrupted.

"I heard piano music. In the family room. So I came down to see who was playing."

My parents were both staring at me as if I were a Martian.

"Didn't you hear it?" I cried.

They shook their heads.

I turned to the piano. No one there. Of course.

I hurried over to the piano bench, leaned down, and rubbed my hand over the surface.

It was warm.

"Someone was sitting here. I can tell!" I exclaimed.

"Not funny," Mum said, making a face.

"Not funny, Jerry," Dad echoed. "You came down here to pull some kind of prank—didn't you!" he accused.

"Huh? Me?"

"Don't play the innocent, Jerome," Mum said, rolling her eyes. "We know you. You're *never* innocent."

"I wasn't joking!" I cried angrily. "I heard music, someone playing—"

"Who?" Dad demanded. "Who was playing?"

"Maybe it was Bonkers," Mum laughed.

Dad laughed too, but I didn't.

"What was the joke, Jerry? What were you planning to do?" Dad asked.

"Were you going to do something to the piano?" Mum demanded, staring at me so hard, I could practically *feel* it. "That's a valuable instrument, you know."

I sighed wearily. I felt so frustrated, I wanted to shout, scream, throw a fit, and maybe slug them both. "The piano is *haunted!*" I shouted.

The words just popped into my head.

"Huh?" It was Dad's turn to give me a hard stare.

"It must be haunted!" I insisted, my voice shaking. "It keeps playing—but there's no one playing it!"

"I've heard enough," Mum muttered, shaking her head. "I'm going back to bed."

"Ghosts, huh?" Dad asked, rubbing his chin thoughtfully. He stepped up to me and lowered his head, the way he does when he's about to unload something serious. "Listen, Jerry, I know this house might seem old and kind of scary. And I know how hard it was for you to leave your friends behind and move away."

"Dad, please—" I interrupted.

But he kept going. "The house is just old, Jerry. Old and a little rundown. That doesn't mean it's haunted. These ghosts of yours—don't you see?—they're really your fears coming out."

Dad has a psychology degree.

"Skip the lecture, Dad," I told him. "I'm going to bed."

"Okay, Jer," he said, patting my shoulder. "Remember—in a few weeks, you'll know I'm right. In a few weeks, this ghost business will all seem silly to you."

Boy, was he wrong!

I slammed my locker shut and started to put on my jacket. The long school corridors echoed with laughing voices, slamming lockers, calls and shouts.

The corridors were always noisier on Friday afternoons. School was over, and the weekend was here!

"Oooh, what's that smell?" I cried, making a disgusted face.

Beside me, a girl was down on her knees, pawing through a pile of junk on the floor of her locker. "I *wondered* where that apple disappeared to!" she exclaimed.

She climbed to her feet, holding a shrivelled, brown apple in one hand. The sour odour invaded my nostrils. I thought I was going to throw up!

I must have been making a funny face, because she burst out laughing. "Hungry?" She pushed the disgusting thing in my face.

"No thanks." I pushed it back towards her. "You can have it."

She laughed again. She was quite pretty. She had long, straight black hair and green eyes.

She put the rotten apple down on the floor. "You're the new kid, right?" she asked. "I'm Kim. Kim Li Chin."

"Hi," I said. I told her my name. "You're in my maths class. And science class," I told her.

She turned back to her locker, searching for more stuff. "I know," she replied. "I saw you fall out of your chair when Miss Klein asked you a question."

"I just did that to be funny," I explained quickly. "I didn't really fall."

"I know," she said. She pulled a heavy grey wool sweater down over her lighter sweater. Then she reached down and removed a black violin case from her locker.

"Is that your lunchbox?" I joked.

"I'm late for my violin lesson," she answered, slamming her locker shut. She struggled to push the padlock closed.

"I'm taking piano lessons," I told her. "Well, I mean I've just started."

"You know, I live opposite you," she said, adjusting her rucksack over her shoulder. "I watched you move in."

"Really?" I replied, surprised. "Well, maybe you could come over and we could play together. I mean, play music. You know. I'm taking lessons every Saturday with Dr Shreek."

Her mouth dropped open in horror as she stared at me. "You're doing *what?*" she cried.

"Taking piano lessons with Dr Shreek," I repeated.

183

"Oh!" She uttered a soft cry, spun round, and began running towards the front door.

"Hey, Kim—" I called after her. "Kim—what's wrong?"

But she had disappeared out of the door.

"Excellent hands. Excellent!" Dr Shreek declared.

"Thanks," I replied awkwardly.

I was seated at the piano bench, hunched over the piano, my hands spread over the keys. Dr Shreek stood beside me, staring down at my hands.

"Now play the piece again," he instructed, raising his blue eyes to mine. His smile faded beneath his white moustache as his expression turned serious. "Play it carefully, my boy. Slowly and carefully. Concentrate on your fingers. Each finger is alive, remember—*alive!*"

"My fingers are alive," I repeated, staring down at them.

What a weird thought, I told myself.

I began to play, concentrating on the notes on the music sheet propped above the keyboard. It was a simple melody, a beginner's piece by Bach.

185

I thought it sounded pretty good.

"The fingers! The fingers!" Dr Shreek cried. He leaned down towards the keyboard, bringing his face close to mine. "Remember, the fingers are alive!"

What's with this guy and fingers? I asked myself.

I finished the piece. I glanced up to see a frown darken his face.

"Pretty good, Jerry," he said softly. "Now let us try it a bit faster."

"I goofed up the middle bit," I confessed.

"You lost your concentration," he replied. He reached down and spread my fingers over the keys. "Again," he instructed. "But faster. And concentrate. Concentrate on your hands."

I took a deep breath and began the piece again. But this time I messed it up immediately.

I started again. It sounded pretty good. Only a few dud notes.

I wondered if Mum and Dad could hear it. Then I remembered they had gone grocery shopping.

Dr Shreek and I were alone in the house.

I finished the piece and lowered my hands to my lap with a sigh.

"Not bad. Now faster," Dr Shreek ordered.

"Maybe we should try another piece," I suggested. "This is getting pretty boring."

"Faster this time," he replied, totally ignoring

me. "The hands, Jerry. Remember the hands. They're alive. Let them breathe!"

Let them breathe?

I stared down at my hands, expecting them to talk back to me!

"Begin," Dr Shreek instructed sternly, leaning over me. "Faster."

Sighing, I began to play again. The same boring tune.

"Faster!" the instructor cried. "Faster, Jerry!"

I played faster. My fingers moved over the keys, pounding them hard. I tried to concentrate on the notes, but I was playing too fast for my eyes to keep up.

"Faster!" Dr Shreek cried excitedly, staring down at the keys. "That's it! Faster, Jerry!"

My fingers were moving so fast, they were a blur!

"Faster! Faster!"

Was I playing the right notes? I couldn't tell. It was too fast, too fast to *hear*!

"Faster, Jerry!" Dr Shreek instructed, screaming at the top of his lungs. "Faster! The hands are alive! Alive!"

"I can't do it!" I cried. "Please—!"

"Faster! Faster!"

"I can't!" I insisted. It was too fast. Too fast to play. Too fast to hear.

I tried to stop.

But my hands kept going!

"Stop! Stop!" I screamed down at them in horror.

"Faster! Play faster!" Dr Shreek ordered, his eyes wide with excitement, his face bright red. "The hands are *alive!*"

"No—please! Stop!" I called down to my hands. "Stop playing!"

But they really *were* alive. They wouldn't stop.

My fingers flew over the keys. A crazy tidal wave of notes flooded the family room.

"Faster! Faster!" the instructor ordered.

And despite my frightened cries to stop, my hands gleefully obeyed him, playing on, faster and faster and faster.

Faster and faster, the music swirled around me.

It's choking me, I thought, gasping for breath. I can't breathe.

I struggled to stop my hands. But they moved frantically over the keys, playing louder. Louder.

My hands began to ache. They throbbed with pain.

But still they played. Faster. Louder.

Until I woke up.

I sat up in bed, wide awake.

And realized I was sitting on my hands.

They both tingled painfully. Pins and needles. My hands had fallen asleep.

I had been asleep. The weird piano lesson—it was a dream.

A strange nightmare.

"It's still Friday night," I said aloud. The sound of my voice helped bring me out of the dream.

I shook my hands, trying to get the circulation going, trying to stop the uncomfortable tingling.

My forehead was sweating, a cold sweat. My whole body felt clammy. The pyjama top stuck damply to my back. I shuddered, suddenly chilled.

And realized the piano music hadn't stopped.

I gasped and gripped the bedcovers tightly. Holding my breath, I listened.

The notes floated into my dark bedroom.

Not the frantic roar of notes from my dream. The slow, sad melody I had heard before.

Still trembling from my frightening dream, I climbed silently out of bed.

The music floated up from the family room, so soft, so mournful.

Who is playing down there?

My hands still tingled as I made my way over the cold floorboards to the doorway. I stopped in the hall and listened.

The tune ended, then began again.

Tonight I am going to solve this mystery, I told myself.

My heart was pounding. My whole body was tingling now. Pins and needles up and down my back.

Ignoring how frightened I felt, I walked quietly down the hall to the staircase. The dim night-light down near the floor made my shadow rise up on the wall.

It startled me for a moment. I hung back. But then I hurried down the stairs, leaning hard on the banister to keep the steps from creaking.

The piano music grew louder as I crossed the dark living room.

Nothing is going to stop me tonight, I told myself. Nothing.

Tonight I am going to see who is playing the piano.

The music continued, soft high notes, so light and sad.

I tiptoed carefully through the living room, holding my breath, listening to the music.

I stepped up to the doorway to the family room.

The music continued, a little louder.

The same melody, over and over again.

Peering into the darkness, I stepped into the room.

One step. Another.

The piano was only a few feet in front of me.

The music was so clear, so close.

But I couldn't see anyone on the piano bench. I couldn't see anyone there at all.

Who is playing? Who is playing this sad, sad music in the darkness?

Trembling all over, I took another step closer. Another step.

"Who—who's there!" I called out in a choked whisper.

I stopped, my hands knotted tensely into tight fists at my sides. I stared hard into the blackness, straining to see.

The music continued. I could hear fingers on the keys, hear the slide of feet on the pedals.

"Who's there? Who's playing?" My voice was tiny and shrill.

There's *no one* here, I realized to my horror.

The piano is playing, but there's *no one* here.

Then, slowly, very slowly, like a grey cloud forming in the night sky, the ghost began to appear.

At first I could just see faint outlines, pale lines of grey moving against the blackness.

I gasped. My heart was pounding so hard, I thought it would burst.

The grey lines took shape, began to fill in.

I stood frozen in terror, too frightened to run or even look away.

And as I stared, a woman came into view. I couldn't tell if she was young or old. She had her head down and her eyes closed, and was concentrating on the piano keys.

She had long, wavy hair hanging loose down to her shoulders. She wore a short-sleeved top and a long skirt. Her face, her skin, her hair—all grey. Everything was grey.

She continued to play as if I weren't standing there.

Her eyes were closed. Her lips formed a sad smile.

She was quite pretty, I realized.

But she was a ghost. A ghost playing the piano in our family room.

"Who are you? What are you doing here?" My high-pitched, tight voice startled me. The words came flying out, almost beyond my control.

She stopped playing and opened her eyes. She stared hard at me, studying me. Her smile faded quickly. Her face revealed no emotion at all.

I stared back, into the grey. It was like looking at someone in a heavy, dark fog.

With the music stopped, the house had become so quiet, so terrifyingly quiet. "Who—who are you?" I repeated, stammering in my tiny voice.

Her grey eyes narrowed in sadness. "This is my house," she said. Her voice was a dry whisper, as dry as dead leaves. As dry as death.

"This is my house." The whispered words seemed to come from far away, so soft I wasn't sure I had heard them.

"I—don't understand," I choked out, feeling a cold chill at the back of my neck. "What are you doing here?"

"My house," came the whispered reply. "My piano."

"But who *are* you?" I repeated. "Are you a *ghost?*"

As I uttered my frightened question, she let out

a loud sigh. And as I stared into the greyness, I saw her face begin to change.

The eyes closed, and her cheeks began to droop. Her grey skin appeared to fall, to melt away. It drooped like biscuit batter, like soft clay. It fell onto her shoulders, then tumbled to the floor. Her hair followed, falling off in thick clumps.

A silent cry escaped my lips as her skull was revealed. Her grey skull.

Nothing remained of her face except for her eyes, her grey eyes, which bulged in the open sockets, staring at me through the darkness.

"*Stay away from my piano!*" she rasped. "*I'm warning you—STAY AWAY!*"

I backed up and turned away from the hideous, rasping skull. I tried to scramble away, but my legs didn't cooperate.

I fell.

Hit the floor on my knees.

I struggled to pull myself up, but I was shaking too hard.

"*Stay away from my piano!*" The grey skull glared at me with its bulging eyes.

"Mum! Dad!" I tried to scream, but it came out a muffled whisper.

I scrambled to my feet, my heart pounding, my throat closed tight with fear.

"*This is my house! My piano! STAY AWAY!*"

"Mum! Help me! Dad!"

This time I managed to call out. "Mum—Dad —please!"

To my relief, I heard bumping and clattering in the hall. Heavy footsteps.

"Jerry? Jerry? Where are you?" Mum called. "Ow!" I heard her bump into something in the dining room.

Dad reached the family room first.

I grabbed him by the shoulders, then pointed. "Dad—look! A ghost! It's a GHOST!"

Dad clicked on the light. Mum stumbled into the room, holding one knee.

I pointed in horror to the piano bench.

Which was now empty.

"The ghost—I saw her!" I cried, shaking all over. I turned to my parents. "Did you hear her? *Did* you?"

"Jerry, calm down." Dad put his hands on my trembling shoulders. "Calm down. It's okay. Everything is okay."

"But did you see her?" I demanded. "She was sitting there, playing the piano, and—"

"Ow. I really hurt my knee," Mum groaned. "I bumped it on the coffee table. Oww."

"Her skin dropped off. Her eyes bulged out of her skull!" I told them. I couldn't get that grinning skull out of my mind. I could still see her, as if her picture had been burned into my eyes.

"There's no one there," Dad said softly,

holding onto my shoulders. "See? No one."

"Did you have a nightmare?" Mum asked, bending to massage her knee.

"It *wasn't* a nightmare!" I screamed. "I *saw* her! I really did! She *talked* to me. She told me this was her piano, her house."

"Let's sit down and talk about this," Mum suggested. "Would you like a cup of hot cocoa?"

"You don't believe me—*do* you?" I cried angrily. "I'm telling you the *truth!*"

"We don't really believe in ghosts," Dad said quietly. He guided me to the red leather sofa against the wall and sat down beside me. Yawning, Mum followed us, lowering herself onto the sofa arm.

"You don't believe in ghosts, do you, Jerry?" Mum asked.

"I do now!" I exclaimed. "Why don't you listen to me? I *heard* her playing the piano. I came downstairs and I saw her. She was a woman. She was all grey. And her face fell off. And her skull showed through. And—and—"

I saw Mum give Dad a look.

Why wouldn't they believe me?

"A woman at work was telling me about a doctor," Mum said softly, reaching down and taking my hand. "A nice doctor who talks to young people. Dr Frye, I think his name was."

"Huh? You mean a psychiatrist?" I cried

shrilly. "You think I'm *crazy?*"

"No, of course not," Mum replied quickly, still holding on to my hand. "I think something has made you very nervous, Jerry. And I don't think it would hurt to talk to someone about it."

"What are you nervous about, Jer?" Dad asked, straightening the collar of his pyjama top. "Is it the new house? Going to a new school?"

"Is it the piano lessons?" Mum asked. "Are you worried about the lessons?" She glanced at the piano, gleaming black and shiny under the ceiling light.

"No. I'm not worried about the lessons," I muttered unhappily. "I *told* you—I'm worried about the *ghost!*"

"I'm going to make you an appointment with Dr Frye," Mum said quietly. "Tell him about the ghost, Jerry. I bet he can explain it all better than your father and I can."

"I'm not mad," I muttered.

"Something has upset you. Something is giving you bad dreams," Dad said. "This doctor will be able to explain it to you." He yawned and stood up, stretching his arms above his head. "I've got to get some sleep."

"Me, too," Mum said, letting go of my hand and climbing off the arm of the sofa. "Do you think you can go to sleep now, Jerry?"

I shook my head and muttered, "I don't know."

"Do you want us to walk you to your room?" she asked.

"I'm not a little baby!" I shouted. I felt angry and frustrated. I wanted to scream and scream until they believed me.

"Well, good night, Jer," Dad said. "Tomorrow's Saturday, so you can sleep late."

"Yeah. Right," I muttered.

"If you have any more bad dreams, wake us up," Mum said.

Dad clicked off the light. They headed down the hall to their room.

I made my way across the living room to the front stairs.

I was so angry, I wanted to hit something or kick something. I was really insulted, too.

But as I climbed the creaking stairs in the darkness, my anger turned to fear.

The ghost had vanished from the family room. What if she was waiting for me up in my room?

What if I walked into my room and the disgusting grey skull with the bulging eyeballs was staring at me from my bed?

The floorboards squeaked and groaned beneath me as I slowly made my way along the passage to my room. I suddenly felt cold all over. My throat tightened. I struggled to breathe.

She's in there. She's in there waiting for me.

I knew it. I knew she'd be there.

And if I scream, if I cry for help, Mum and Dad will just think I'm crazy.

What does the ghost want?

Why does she play the piano every night? Why did she try to frighten me? Why did she tell me to stay away?

The questions rolled through my mind. I couldn't answer them. I was too tired, too frightened to think clearly.

I hesitated outside my room, breathing hard.

Then, holding onto the wall, I gathered my courage and stepped inside.

As I moved into the darkness, the ghost rose up in front of my bed.

I uttered a choked cry and staggered back to the doorway.

Then I realized I was staring at my covers. I must have kicked them over the foot of the bed during my nightmare about Dr Shreek. They were lying in a heap on the floor.

My heart pounding, I crept back into the room, grabbed the blanket and sheet, and pulled them back onto the bed.

Maybe I *am* cracking up! I thought.

No way, I assured myself. I might be scared and frustrated and angry—but I saw what I saw.

Shivering, I slid into bed and pulled the covers up to my chin. I closed my eyes and tried to force the picture of the ugly grey skull from my mind.

When I finally started to drift off to sleep, I heard the piano music start again.

Dr Shreek arrived promptly at two the next afternoon. Mum and Dad were out in the garage, unpacking more boxes. I took Dr Shreek's coat, then led him into the family room.

It was a cold, blustery day outside, threatening snow. Dr Shreek's cheeks were pink from the cold. With his white hair and moustache, and round belly under his baggy, white shirt, he looked more like Santa Claus than ever.

He rubbed his pudgy hands together to warm them and motioned for me to take a seat at the piano bench. "Such a beautiful instrument," he said cheerily, running a hand over the shiny, black top of the piano. "You are a very lucky young man to find this waiting for you."

"I suppose so," I replied without enthusiasm.

I had slept till eleven, but I was still tired. And I couldn't shake the ghost and her warning from my mind.

"Have you practised your chords?" Dr Shreek asked, leaning against the piano, turning the pages of the music workbook.

"A little," I told him.

"Let me see what you have learned. Here." He began to place my fingers over the keys. "Remember? This is where you start."

I played a scale.

"Excellent hands," Dr Shreek said, smiling. "Keep repeating it, please."

The lesson went well. He kept telling me how good I was, even though I was just playing notes and a simple scale.

Maybe I *do* have some talent, I thought.

I asked him when I could begin learning some rock riffs.

He chuckled for some reason. "In due course," he replied, staring at my hands.

I heard Mum and Dad come in through the kitchen door. A few seconds later, Mum appeared in the living room, rubbing the arms of her sweater. "It's really getting cold out there," she said, smiling at Dr Shreek. "I think it's going to snow."

"It's nice and warm in here," he replied, returning her smile.

"How's the lesson going?" Mum asked him.

"Very well," Dr Shreek told her, winking at me. "I think Jerry shows a lot of promise. I would like him to start taking his lessons at my school."

"That's wonderful!" Mum exclaimed. "Do you really think he has talent?"

"He has excellent hands," Dr Shreek replied.

Something about the way he said it gave me a cold chill.

"Do you teach rock music at your school?" I asked.

He patted my shoulder. "We teach all kinds of

music. My school is very large, and we have many fine instructors. We have pupils of all ages there. Do you think you could come after school on Fridays?"

"That would be fine," Mum said.

Dr Shreek crossed the room and handed my mum a card. "Here is the address of my school. I'm afraid it is at the other end of town."

"No problem," Mum said, studying the card. "I get off work early on Fridays. I can drive him."

"That will end our lesson for today, Jerry," Dr Shreek said. "Practise the new chords. And I'll see you on Friday."

He followed my mum to the living room. I heard them chatting quietly, but I couldn't make out what they were saying.

I stood up and walked to the window. It had started to snow, very large flakes coming down really hard. The snow was already starting to stick.

Staring into the back garden, I wondered if there were any good hills to go sledging on in New Goshen. And I wondered if my sledge had been unpacked.

I cried out when the piano suddenly started to play.

Loud, jangling noise. Like someone pounding furiously on the keys with heavy fists.

Pound. Pound. Pound.

"Jerry—stop it!" Mum shouted from the living room.

"I'm not doing it!" I cried.

Dr Frye's office wasn't the way I imagined a
psychiatrist's office. It was small and bright.
The walls were yellow, and there were colourful
pictures of parrots and toucans and other birds
hanging all around.

He didn't have a black leather couch like
psychiatrists always have on TV and in films.
Instead, he had two soft-looking, green arm-
chairs. He didn't even have a desk. Just the two
chairs.

I sat in one, and he sat in the other.

He was a lot younger than I thought he'd be.
He looked younger than my dad. He had wavy
red hair, slicked down with some kind of gel or
something, I think. And he had a face full of
freckles.

He just didn't look like a psychiatrist at
all.

"Tell me about your new house," he said. He
had his legs crossed. He rested his long notepad

on them as he studied me.

"It's a big, old house," I told him. "That's about it."

He asked me to describe my room, so I did.

Then we talked about the house we'd moved from and my old room. Then we talked about my friends at my old home. Then we talked about my new school.

I felt nervous at first. But he seemed okay. He listened carefully to everything I said. And he didn't give me funny looks, as if I was crazy or something.

Even when I told him about the ghost.

He scribbled down a few notes when I told him about the piano playing late at night. He stopped writing when I told him how I'd seen the ghost, and how her hair fell off and then her face, and how she had screamed at me to stay away.

"My parents didn't believe me," I said, squeezing the soft arms of the chair. My hands were sweating.

"It's a pretty weird story," Dr Frye replied. "If you were your mum and dad, and your kid told you that story, would *you* believe it?"

"Of course," I said. "If it was true."

He chewed on his pencil rubber and stared at me.

"Do you think I'm crazy?" I asked.

He lowered his notepad. He didn't smile at the question. "No. I don't think you're crazy, Jerry. But the human mind can be really strange sometimes."

Then he launched into this long lecture about how sometimes we're afraid of something, but we don't admit to ourselves that we're afraid. So our mind does all kinds of things to show that we're afraid, even though we keep telling ourselves that we're *not* afraid.

In other words, he didn't believe me, either.

"Moving to a new house creates all kinds of stress," he said. "It is possible to start imagining that we see things, that we hear things—just so we don't admit to ourselves what we're *really* afraid of."

"I didn't imagine the piano music," I said. "I can hum the melody for you. And I didn't imagine the ghost. I can tell you just what she looked like."

"Let's talk about it next week," he said, getting to his feet. "Our time is up. But until next time, I just want to assure you that your mind is perfectly normal. You're not crazy, Jerry. You shouldn't think that for a second."

He shook my hand. "You'll see," he said, opening the door for me. "You'll be amazed at what we work out is behind that ghost of yours."

I muttered thanks and walked out of his office.

I made my way through the empty waiting room and stepped into the hallway.

And then I felt the ghost's icy grip tighten around my neck.

The unearthly cold shot through my whole body.

Uttering a terrified cry, I jerked away and spun round to face her.

"Mum!" I cried, my voice shrill and tiny.

"Sorry my hands are so cold," she replied calmly, unaware of how badly she had scared me. "It's *freezing* out. Didn't you hear me calling you?"

"No," I told her. My neck still tingled. I tried to rub the cold away. "I . . . uh . . . was thinking about something, and—"

"Well, I didn't mean to scare you," she said, leading the way across the small car park to the car. She stopped to pull the car keys from her bag. "Did you and Dr Frye have a nice talk?"

"Sort of," I said.

This ghost has me jumping out of my skin, I realized as I climbed into the car. Now I'm seeing the ghost *everywhere*.

I have *got* to calm down, I told myself. I've just *got* to.

I've got to stop thinking that the ghost is following me.

But how?

Friday after school, Mum drove me to Dr Shreek's music school. It was a cold, grey day. I stared at my breath steaming up the passenger window as we drove. It had snowed the day before, and the roads were still icy, and slick.

"I hope we're not late," Mum fretted. We stopped for a light. She cleared the windscreen in front of her with the back of her gloved hand. "I'm afraid to drive any faster than this."

All of the cars were inching along. We drove past a crowd of kids building a snow fort in a front garden. One red-faced little kid was crying because the others wouldn't let him join them.

"The school is practically in the next town," Mum remarked, pumping the brakes as we slid towards a junction. "I wonder why Dr Shreek has his school so far away from every-thing."

"I don't know," I answered dully. I was quite nervous. "Do you think Dr Shreek will be my instructor? Or do you think I'll have someone else?"

Mum shrugged her shoulders. She leaned forward over the steering wheel, struggling to see through the steamed-up windscreen.

Finally, we turned onto the street where the school was located. I stared out at the street of dark, old houses. The houses gave way to woods, the bare trees tilting up under a white blanket of snow.

On the other side of the woods stood a brick building, half-hidden behind tall hedges. "This must be the school," Mum said, stopping the car in the middle of the street and staring up at the old building. "There's no sign or anything. But it's the only building for streets."

"It's creepy-looking," I said.

Squinting through the windscreen, she pulled the car into the narrow gravel drive, nearly hidden by the tall, snow-covered hedges.

"Are you sure this is it?" I asked. I cleared a spot on the window with my hand and peered through it. The old building looked more like a prison than a school. It had rows of tiny windows above the ground floor, and the windows were all barred. Thick ivy covered the front of the building, making it appear even darker than it was.

"I'm fairly sure," Mum said, biting her lip. She lowered the window and stuck her head out, gazing up at the enormous, old house.

The sound of piano music floated into the car. Notes and scales and melodies all mixed together.

"Yeah. We've found it!" Mum declared happily. "Go on, Jerry. Hurry. You're late. I'm going to go and pick up something for dinner. I'll be back in an hour."

I pushed open the car door and stepped out onto the snowy drive. My boots crunched loudly as I started to jog towards the building.

The piano music grew louder. Scales and songs jumbled together into a deafening rumble of noise.

A narrow walk led up to the front entrance. The walk hadn't been shovelled, and a layer of ice had formed under the snow. I slipped and nearly fell as I approached the entrance.

I stopped and gazed up. It looks more like a haunted house than a music school, I thought with a shiver.

Why did I have such a heavy feeling of dread?

Just nervous, I told myself.

Shrugging away my feeling, I turned the cold brass doorknob and pushed the heavy door. It creaked open slowly. Taking a deep breath, I stepped into the school.

A long, narrow corridor stretched before me. The corridor was surprisingly dark. Coming in from the bright, white snow, it took my eyes a long time to adjust.

The walls were a dark tile. My boots thudded noisily on the hard floor. Piano notes echoed through the corridor. The music seemed to burst out from all directions.

Where is Dr Shreek's office? I wondered.

I made my way down the corridor. The lights grew dimmer. I turned into another long corridor, and the piano music grew louder.

There were dark brown doors on both sides of this corridor. The doors had small, round windows in them. As I continued walking, I glanced into the windows.

I could see smiling instructors in each room, their heads bobbing in rhythm to piano music.

Searching for the office, I passed door after door. Each room had a pupil and an instructor inside. The piano sounds became a roar, like an ocean of music crashing against the dark tiled walls.

Dr Shreek really has a lot of pupils, I thought. There must be a hundred pianos playing at once!

I turned another corner and then another.

I suddenly realized I had completely lost my sense of direction. I had no idea where I was. I couldn't find my way back to the front door if I wanted to!

"Dr Shreek, where are you?" I muttered to myself. My voice was drowned out by the booming piano music that echoed off the walls and low ceiling.

I began to feel a little frightened.

What if these dark walls twisted on forever? I imagined myself walking and walking for the rest of my life, unable to find my way out, deafened by the pounding piano music.

"Jerry, stop scaring yourself," I said aloud.

Something caught my eye. I stopped walking and stared up at the ceiling. A small, black camera was perched above my head.

It appeared to be a video camera, like the security cameras you see in banks and shops.

Was someone watching me on a TV screen somewhere?

If they were, why didn't they come and help me find the way to Dr Shreek?

I began to get angry. What kind of school *was*

this? No signs. No office. No one to greet people.

As I turned another corner, I heard a strange thumping sound. At first I thought it was just another piano in one of the practice rooms.

The thumping grew louder, closer. I stopped in the middle of the corridor and listened. A high-pitched whine rose up over the thumping sounds.

Louder. Louder.

The floor seemed to shake.

And as I stared down the corridor, an enormous monster turned the corner. Its huge, square body glowed in the dim light as if it were made of metal. Its rectangular head bobbed near the ceiling.

Its feet crashed against the hard floor as it moved to attack me. Eyes on the sides of its head flashed an angry red.

"No!" I cried, swallowing hard.

It uttered its high-pitched whine in reply. Then it lowered its gleaming head as if preparing for battle.

I spun away, determined to escape.

To my shock, as I turned, I saw Dr Shreek.

He stood just a few metres down the hall. Dr Shreek was watching the enormous creature move in on me, a pleased grin on his face.

I stopped short with a loud gasp.

Behind me, the creature was stomping closer, blasting out its angry whine.

Ahead of me, Dr Shreek, his blue eyes glowing with pleasure, blocked my escape.

I cried out, preparing to be caught from behind by the silvery monster.

But it stopped.

Silence.

No crashing of its heavy metallic feet. No shrill whine.

"Hello, Jerry," Dr Shreek said calmly, still grinning. "What are you doing all the way back here?"

Breathing hard, I pointed to the monster, which stood silently, staring down at me. "I—I—"

"You are admiring our floor sweeper?" Dr Shreek asked.

"Your *what*?" I managed to choke out.

"Our floor sweeper. It *is* rather special," Dr Shreek said. He stepped past me and put a hand on the front of the thing.

"It—it's a machine?" I stammered.

He laughed. "You didn't think it was alive, did you?"

I just gaped at it. I was still too freaked out to speak.

"Mr Toggle, our caretaker, built this for us," Dr Shreek said, rubbing his hand along the square metal front of it. "It works like a dream. Mr Toggle can build anything. He's a genius, a true genius."

"Wh-why does it have a face?" I asked, hanging back against the wall. "Why does it have eyes that light up?"

"Just Mr Toggle's sense of humour," Dr Shreek replied, chuckling. "He put in those cameras, too." He pointed to the video camera perched on the ceiling. "Mr Toggle is a mechanical genius. We couldn't do a thing without him. We really couldn't."

I took a few reluctant steps forward and admired the floor sweeper from closer up. "I—I couldn't find your office," I told Dr Shreek. "I was wandering and wandering—"

"I apologize," he replied quickly. "Let us begin your lesson. Come."

I followed him as he led the way back in the direction I had come. He walked stiffly but

219

rapidly. His white shirt was untucked in front of his big stomach. He swung his hands stiffly as he walked.

I felt really stupid. Imagine letting myself be terrified by a floor sweeper!

He pushed open one of the brown doors with a round window, and I followed him into the room. I glanced quickly around. It was a small, square room lighted by two rows of fluorescent lights on the ceiling. There was no window.

The only furniture was a small, brown upright piano, a narrow piano bench, and a music stand.

Dr Shreek motioned for me to sit down on the piano bench, and we began our lesson. He stood behind me, placing my fingers carefully on the keys, even though I now knew how to do it myself.

We practised different notes. I hit C's and D's. Then we tried E's and F's. He showed me my first chord. Then he made me do scales over and over again.

"Excellent!" he declared near the end of the hour. "Excellent work, Jerry. I'm most pleased!" His Santa Claus cheeks were bright pink beneath his white moustache.

I squeezed my hands together, trying to get rid of a cramp. "Are you going to be my teacher?" I asked.

He nodded. "Yes, I will instruct you in the

basics," he replied. "Then when your hands are ready, you will be given over to one of our fine teachers."

When my hands are ready?

What exactly did he mean by that?

"Let us try this short piece," he said, reaching over me to turn the page in the music book. "Now, this piece has only three notes. But you must pay attention to the quarter notes and the half notes. Do you remember how long to hold a half note?"

I demonstrated on the piano. Then I tried to play the short melody. I did pretty well. Only a few naff notes.

"Wonderful! Wonderful!" Dr Shreek declared, staring at my hands as I played. He glanced at his watch. "I'm afraid our time is up. See you next Friday, Jerry. Be sure to practise what I've showed you."

I thanked him and climbed to my feet. I was glad the lesson was over. Having to concentrate so hard was really tiring. Both my hands were sweating, and I still had a cramp in one.

I headed for the door, then stopped. "Which way do I go?" I asked. "How do I get to the front?"

Dr Shreek was busy collecting the work sheets we had used, tucking them into the music book. "Just keep going left," he said without looking up. "You can't miss it."

I said goodbye and stepped out into the dark hallway. My ears were immediately attacked by the roar of the piano notes.

Aren't the other lessons over? I wondered.

How come they keep playing them even though the hour is up?

I glanced in both directions, making sure there were no floor sweepers waiting to attack. Then I turned left, as Dr Shreek had instructed, and began to follow the corridor towards the front.

As I passed door after door, I could see the smiling instructors inside each room, their heads moving in rhythm with the piano playing.

Most of the pupils in these rooms were more advanced than me, I realized. They weren't practising notes and scales. They were playing long, complicated pieces.

I turned left, then when the corridor came to an end, turned left one more time.

It took me a while to realize that I was lost again.

Had I missed a left turn somewhere?

The dark halls with their rows of brown doors on both sides all looked alike.

I turned left again. My heart began to pound. Why wasn't anyone else in the hall?

Then up ahead I saw double doors. The front exit must be through those doors, I decided.

I made my way eagerly to the double doors and started to push through them—when powerful hands grabbed me from behind, and a gruff voice rasped in my ear, "No, you don't!"

"Huh?" I uttered a silent cry.

The hands pulled me back, then let go of my shoulders.

The double doors swung back into place.

I spun round to see a tall, wiry man with long, scraggly black hair and a stubbly black beard. He wore a yellow T-shirt under denim dungarees.

"Not that way," he said softly. "You're looking for the front? It's up there." He pointed to the hall to the left.

"Oh. Sorry," I said, breathing hard. "You . . . scared me."

The man apologized. "I'll take you to the front," he offered, scratching his stubbly cheek. "Allow me to introduce myself. I'm Mr Toggle."

"Oh. Hi," I said. "I'm Jerry Hawkins. Dr Shreek told me about you. I—I saw your floor sweeper."

He smiled. His black eyes lit up like dark coals. "It's a beauty, isn't it? I have a few other creations like it, some even better."

"Dr Shreek says you're a mechanical genius," I gushed.

Mr Toggle chuckled to himself. "Yes. I programmed him to say that!" he joked. We both laughed.

"Next time you come to the school, I'll show you some of my other inventions," Mr Toggle offered, adjusting his dungaree straps over his slender shoulders.

"Thanks," I replied. The front door was right up ahead. I was never so glad to see a door! "I'm sure I'll catch on to the layout of this place," I said.

He didn't seem to hear me. "Dr Shreek tells me you have excellent hands," he said, a strange smile forming under his stubbly black beard. "That's what we look for here, Jerry. That's what we look for."

Feeling sort of awkward, I thanked him. I mean, what are you supposed to say when someone tells you what excellent hands you've got?

I pushed open the heavy front door and saw Mum waiting in the car. "Good night!" I called, and eagerly ran out of the school, into the snowy evening.

After dinner, Mum and Dad insisted that I show them what I had learned in my piano lesson. I didn't really want to. I had only learned that one simple song, and I still hadn't played it all the way through without making any mistakes.

But they forced me into the family room and pushed me onto the piano bench. "If I'm going to pay for the lessons, I want to hear what you're learning," Dad said. He sat down close to Mum on the sofa, facing the back of the piano.

"We only tried one song," I said. "Couldn't we wait till I learn some more?"

"Play it," Dad ordered.

I sighed. "I've got cramp in my hand."

"Come on, Jerry. Don't make excuses," Mum snapped immediately. "Just play the song, okay? Then we won't bug you any more to-night."

"What did the school look like?" Dad asked Mum. "It's right over on the other side of town, isn't it?"

"It's practically *out* of town," Mum told him. "It's in this very old house. Sort of run-down looking, actually. But Jerry told me it's nice inside."

"No, I didn't," I interrupted. "I said it was big. I didn't say it was nice. I got lost in the corridors twice!"

Dad laughed. "I see you have your mother's sense of direction!"

226

Mum gave Dad a playful shove. "Just play the piece," she said to me.

I found it in the music book and propped the book in front of me on the piano. Then I arranged my fingers on the keys and prepared to play.

But before I hit the first note, the piano erupted with a barrage of low notes. It sounded as if someone was pounding on the keys with both fists.

"Jerry—stop it," Mum said sharply. "That's too loud."

"That can't be what you learned," Dad added.

I put my fingers in place and began to play.

But my notes were drowned out by the horrible, loud banging again.

It sounded like a little kid pounding away on the keys as hard as he could.

"Jerry—give us a *break!*" Mum shouted, holding her ears.

"But I'm not *doing* it!" I screamed. "It isn't *me!*"

They didn't believe me.

Instead, they got angry. They accused me of never taking anything seriously, and sent me up to my room.

I was actually glad to get out of the family room and away from that haunted piano. I knew who was pounding the keys and making that racket. The ghost was doing it.

Why? What was she trying to prove?

What did she plan to do to me?

Those questions I couldn't answer . . . yet.

The next Friday afternoon, Mr Toggle kept his promise. He greeted me at the door to the piano school after my mum had dropped me off. He led me through the twisting corridor to his enormous workshop.

Mr Toggle's workshop was the size of a sports hall. The vast room was cluttered with machines and electronic equipment.

An enormous two-headed metal creature, at least three times as tall as the floor sweeper that had terrified me the week before, stood in the centre. It was surrounded by tape machines, stacks of electric motors, cases of tools and strange-looking parts, video equipment, a pile of bicycle wheels, several piano frames with no insides, animal cages, and an old car with its seats removed.

One entire wall seemed to be a control panel. It had more than a dozen video screens, all on, all showing different classes going on in the school. Around the screens were thousands of dials and knobs, blinking red and green lights, speakers, and microphones.

Beneath the control panel, on a counter that ran the length of the room, stood at least a dozen computers. All of them seemed to be powered up.

"Wow!" I exclaimed. My eyes kept darting from one amazing thing to another. "I don't *believe* this!"

Mr Toggle chuckled. His dark eyes lit up. "I find ways to keep busy," he said. He led me to an uncluttered corner of the enormous room. "Let me show you some of my musical instruments."

He walked to a row of tall, grey metal cabinets along the far wall. He pulled a few items from a cabinet and came hurrying back.

"Do you know what this is, Jerry?" He held

up a shiny, brass instrument attached to some kind of tank.

"A saxophone?" I guessed.

"A very special saxophone," he said, grinning. "See? It's attached to this tank of compressed air. That means you don't have to blow into it. You can concentrate on your fingering."

"Wow," I said. "That's really neat."

"Here. Put this on," Mr Toggle urged. He slipped a brown leather cap over my head. The cap had several thin wires flowing out of the back, and it was attached to a small keyboard.

"What is it?" I asked, adjusting the cap over my ears.

"Blink your eyes," Mr Toggle instructed.

I blinked my eyes, and the keyboard played a chord. I moved my eyes from right to left. It played another chord. I winked one eye. It played a note.

"It's completely eye-controlled," Mr Toggle said with pride. "No hands required."

"Wow," I repeated. I didn't know what else to say. This stuff was amazing!

Mr Toggle glanced up at a row of clocks on the control panel wall. "You're late for class, Jerry. Dr Shreek will be waiting. Tell him it's my fault, okay?"

"Okay," I said. "Thanks for showing me everything."

He laughed. "I didn't show you *everything*," he joked. "There's lots more." He rubbed his stubbly beard. "But you'll see it all in due course."

I thanked him again and hurried towards the door. It was nearly four-fifteen. I hoped Dr Shreek wouldn't be angry that I was fifteen minutes late.

As I jogged across the enormous workshop, I nearly ran into a row of dark metal cabinets, shut and padlocked.

Turning away from them, I suddenly heard a voice.

"Help!" A weak cry.

I stopped by the side of the cabinet and listened hard.

And heard it again. A little voice, very faint. "Help me, please!"

"Mr Toggle—what's that?" I cried.

He had begun fiddling with the wires on the brown leather cap. He slowly looked up. "What's *what*?"

"That cry," I told him, pointing to the cabinet. "I heard a voice."

He frowned. "It's just damaged equipment," he muttered, returning his attention to the wires.

"Huh? Damaged equipment?" I wasn't sure I had heard him correctly.

"Yeah. Just some damaged equipment," he repeated immediately. "You'd better hurry, Jerry. Dr Shreek must be wondering where you are."

I heard a second cry. A voice, very weak and tiny. "Help me—please!"

I hesitated. Mr Toggle was staring at me impatiently.

I had no choice. I turned and ran from the

232

room, the weak cries still in my ears.

On Saturday afternoon I went outside to shovel snow off our drive. It had snowed the night before, only a centimetre or two. Now it was one of those clear winter days with a bright blue sky overhead.

It felt good to be out in the crisp air, getting some exercise. Everything seemed so fresh and clean.

I was finishing down at the bottom of the drive, my arms starting to ache from all the shovelling, when I saw Kim Li Chin. She was climbing out of her mother's black Honda, carrying her violin case. I realized she was coming from a lesson.

I had seen her at school a few times, but I hadn't really talked to her since that day she'd run away from me in the corridor.

"Hey!" I called across the street, leaning on the shovel, a little out of beath. "Hi!"

She handed the violin case to her mother and waved back. Then she came jogging towards me, her black shoes crunching over the snow. "How's it going?" she asked. "Pretty snow, huh?"

I nodded. "Yeah. Want to shovel some? I still have to do the path."

She laughed. "No thanks." She had a high, tinkly laugh, like two glasses clinking together.

"You coming from a violin lesson?" I asked, still leaning on the shovel.

"Yeah. I'm working on a Bach piece. It's pretty hard."

"You're ahead of me," I told her. "I'm still doing mostly notes and scales."

Her smile faded. Her eyes grew thoughtful.

We talked for a little while about school. Then I asked if she'd like to come in and have some hot chocolate or something.

"What about the path?" she asked, pointing. "I thought you had to shovel it."

"Dad would be disappointed if I didn't save some of it for him," I joked.

Mum filled two big white mugs with hot chocolate. Of course I burned my tongue on the first sip.

Kim and I were sitting in the family room. Kim sat on the piano bench and tapped some keys lightly. "It has a really good tone," she said, her face growing serious. "Better than my mother's piano."

"Why did you run away that afternoon?" I blurted out.

It had been on my mind ever since it happened. I *had* to know the answer.

She lowered her eyes to the piano keys and pretended she hadn't heard me.

So I asked again. "Why did you run away like that, Kim?"

"I didn't," she replied finally, still avoiding my eyes. "I was late for a lesson, that's all."

I put my hot chocolate mug down on the coffee table and leaned against the arm of the sofa. "I told you I was going to take piano lessons at the Shreek School, remember? Then you got this strange look on your face, and you ran away."

Kim sighed. She had the hot chocolate mug in her lap. I saw that she was gripping it tightly in both hands. "Jerry, I really don't want to talk about it," she said softly. "It's too . . . too scary."

"Scary?" I asked.

"Don't you *know* the stories about the Shreek School?" she asked.

I laughed. I'm not sure why. Maybe it was the serious expression on Kim's face. "Stories? What kind of stories?"

"I really don't want to tell you," she said. She took a long sip from the white mug, then returned it to her lap.

"I've just moved here, remember?" I told her. "So I haven't heard any stories. What are they about?"

"Things about the school," she muttered. She climbed off the piano bench and walked to the window, carrying the mug in one hand.

"What kinds of things?" I demanded. "Come on, Kim—*tell* me!"

"Well . . . things like, there are monsters there," she replied, staring out of the window into my snowy back garden. "Real monsters that live in the basement."

"Monsters?" I laughed.

Kim spun round. "It's not funny," she snapped.

"I've *seen* the monsters," I told her, shaking my head.

Her face filled with surprise. "You've *what?*"

"I've seen the monsters," I repeated. "They're floor sweepers."

"Huh?" Her mouth dropped open. She nearly spilled hot chocolate down the front of her sweatshirt. "Floor sweepers?"

"Yeah. Mr Toggle built them. He works at the school. He's some kind of mechanical genius. He builds all kinds of things."

"But—" she started.

"I saw one on my first day at the school," I continued. "I thought it was some kind of monster. It made this weird whining sound, and it was coming right at me. I practically dropped my teeth! But it was one of Mr Toggle's floor cleaners."

Kim tilted her head, staring at me thoughtfully. "Well, you know how stories get started," she said. "I *knew* they probably weren't true. They probably all have simple explanations like that."

"All?" I asked. "Are there more?"

"Well . . ." She hesitated. "There were stories about how kids went in for lessons and never came out again. How they vanished, just disappeared."

"That's impossible," I said.

"Yeah, I suppose so," she agreed quickly.

Then I remembered the tiny voice from the cabinet, calling out for help.

It *had* to be some invention of Mr Toggle's, I told myself. It *had* to be.

Damaged equipment, he'd said. He didn't seem in the least bit excited or upset about it.

"It's funny how scary stories get started," Kim said, walking back to the piano bench.

"Well, the piano school building is creepy and old," I said. "It really looks like some sort of haunted mansion. I suppose that's probably why some of the stories got started."

"Probably," she agreed.

"The school isn't haunted, but that piano is!" I told her. I don't know what made me say it. I hadn't told anyone about the ghost and the piano. I knew no one would believe me.

Kim gave a little start and stared at the piano. "This piano is haunted? What do you mean? How do you know?"

"Late at night, I hear someone playing it," I told her. "A woman. I saw her once."

Kim laughed. "You're having me on—right?"

I shook my head. "No, I'm serious, Kim. I saw this woman. Late at night. She plays the same sad tune over and over again."

"Jerry, come on!" Kim pleaded, rolling her eyes.

"The woman talked to me. Her skin fell off. It—it was so frightening, Kim. Her face disappeared. Her skull, it stared at me. And she warned me to stay away. Stay away."

I felt a shiver. Somehow I had shut that scary scene out of my mind for a few days. But now, as I told it to Kim, it all came back to me.

Kim had a big grin on her face. "You're a better storyteller than I am," she said. "Do you know a lot of ghost stories?"

"*It isn't a story!*" I cried. Suddenly, I was desperate for her to believe me.

Kim started to reply, but my mum poked her head into the living room and interrupted. "Kim, your mum just phoned. She needs you to come home now."

"Suppose I'd better go," Kim said, putting down the hot chocolate mug.

I followed her out.

We had just reached the family room doorway when the piano began to play. A strange jumble of notes.

"See?" I cried excitedly to Kim. "See? *Now* do you believe me?"

21

We both turned back to stare at the piano.

Bonkers was strutting over the keys, his tail straight up behind him.

Kim laughed. "Jerry, you're funny! I almost believed you!"

"But—but—but—" I spluttered.

That stupid cat had made a fool of me again.

"See you at school," Kim said. "I loved your ghost story."

"Thanks," I said weakly. Then I hurried across the room to chase Bonkers off the piano.

Late that night I heard the piano playing again.

I sat up straight in bed. The shadows on my ceiling seemed to be moving in time to the music.

I had been sleeping lightly, restlessly. I must have kicked off my covers in my sleep, because they were bunched at the foot of the bed.

Now, listening to the familiar slow tune, I was wide awake.

This was not Bonkers strutting over the keys. This was the ghost.

I stood up. The floorboards were ice-cold. Outside the bedroom window, I could see the winter-bare trees shivering in a strong breeze.

As I crept to the bedroom doorway, the music grew louder.

Should I go down there? I asked myself.

Will the ghost disappear the minute I poke my head into the family room?

Do I really want to see her?

I didn't want to see that hideous, grinning skull again.

But I realized I couldn't just stand there in the doorway. I couldn't go back to bed. I couldn't ignore it.

I *had* to go and investigate.

I was pulled downstairs, as if tugged by an invisible rope.

Maybe this time Mum and Dad will hear her, too, I thought as I made my way along the landing. Maybe they will see her, too. Maybe they will finally believe me.

Kim flashed into my mind as I started down the creaking stairs. She thought I was making up a ghost story. She thought I was trying to be funny.

But there really was a ghost in my house, a ghost playing my piano. And I was the only one who knew it.

Into the living room. Across the worn carpet to the dining room.

The music floated so gently, so quietly.

Such ghostly music, I thought . . .

I hesitated just outside the family room doorway. Would she vanish the instant I peeped in?

Was she *waiting* for me?

Taking a deep breath, I took a step into the family room.

She had her head down, her long hair falling over her face.

I couldn't see her eyes.

The piano music seemed to swirl around me, pulling me closer despite my fear.

My legs were trembling, but I took a step closer. Then another.

She was all grey. Shades of grey against the blackness of the night sky through the windows.

Her head bobbed and swayed in rhythm with the music. The sleeves of her blouse billowed as her arms moved over the keys.

I couldn't see her eyes. I couldn't see her face. Her long hair covered her, as if hiding her behind a curtain.

The music soared, so sad, so incredibly sad.

I took a step closer. I suddenly realized I had forgotten to breathe. I let my breath out in a loud *whoosh*.

She stopped playing. Maybe the sound of my

breathing alerted her that I was there.

As she raised her head, I could see her pale eyes peering out at me through her hair.

I didn't move.

I didn't breathe.

I didn't make a sound.

"The stories are true," she whispered. A dry whisper that seemed to come from far away.

I wasn't sure I had heard her correctly. I tried to say something, but my voice caught in my throat.

No sound came out at all.

"The stories are true," she repeated. Her voice was only air, a hiss of air.

I goggled at her.

"Wh-what stories?" I finally managed to choke out.

"The stories about the school," she answered, her hair falling over her face. Then she started to raise her arms off the piano keys. "*They're true*," she moaned. "*The stories are true*."

She held her arms up to me.

Gaping at them in horror, I cried out—then started to gag.

Her arms ended in stumps. She had no hands.

The next thing I knew, my mum was wrapping her arms around me. "Jerry, calm down. Jerry, it's okay. It's okay," she kept repeating.

"Huh? Mum?"

I was gasping for breath. My chest was heaving up and down. My legs were all wobbly.

"Mum? Where—? How—?"

I looked up to see my dad standing a few metres away, squinting at me through his glasses, his arms crossed in front of his bathrobe. "Jerry, you were screaming loud enough to wake the whole neighbourhood!"

I stared at him in disbelief. I hadn't even realized I was screaming.

"It's okay, now," Mum said soothingly. "It's okay, Jerry. You're okay now."

I'm okay?

Again, I pictured the ghost woman, all in grey, her hair falling down, forming a curtain over her face. Again, I saw her raise her arms to show me.

Again, I saw the horrible stumps where her hands should have been.

And again, I heard her dry whisper, "*The stories are true.*"

Why didn't she have any hands? Why?

How could she play the piano without hands?

Why was she haunting my piano? Why did she want to terrify me?

The questions circled my brain so fast, I wanted to scream and scream and scream. But I was all screamed out.

"Your mum and I were both sound asleep. You scared us to death," Dad said. "I've never heard wails like that."

I didn't remember screaming. I didn't remember the ghost disappearing, or Mum and Dad rushing in.

It was too horrifying. I think my mind just shut off.

"I'll make you some hot chocolate," Mum said, still holding me tight. "Try to stop trembling."

"I—I'm trying," I stammered.

"It must have been another nightmare," I heard Dad tell Mum. "A vivid one."

"It wasn't a nightmare!" I shrieked.

"Sorry," Dad said quickly. He didn't want to get me started again.

But it was too late. Before I even realized it was happening, I started to scream. "I don't want to play the piano! Get it out of here! Get it out!"

"Jerry, please—" Mum pleaded, her face tight with alarm.

But I couldn't stop. "I don't want to play! I don't want lessons! I won't go to that piano school! I won't, I *won't!*"

"Okay, okay!" Dad cried, shouting to be heard over my desperate wails. "Okay, Jerry. No one is going to force you."

"Huh?" I gazed from one parent to the other, trying to see if they were serious.

"If you don't want piano lessons, you don't have to take them," Mum said, keeping her voice in a low, soothing tone. "You're only signed up for one more anyway."

"Yeah," Dad quickly joined in. "When you go to the school on Friday, just tell Dr Shreek that it's your last lesson."

"But I don't want—" I started.

Mum put a gentle hand over my mouth. "You have to tell Dr Shreek, Jerry. You can't just give up."

"Tell him on Friday," Dad urged. "You don't have to play the piano if you don't want to. Really."

Mum's eyes searched mine. "Does that make you feel better, Jerry?"

I glanced at the piano, now silent, shimmering dully in the dim light from overhead. "Yeah. I suppose so," I muttered uncertainly. "I suppose it does."

On Friday afternoon after school, a grey, blustery day with dark snowclouds hovering low overhead, Mum drove me to the piano school. She pulled into the long drive between the tall hedges and stopped in front of the entrance to the dark, old building.

I hesitated. "Couldn't I just run in and tell Dr Shreek that I'm not coming any more, then run right back out?"

Mum glanced at the clock on the dashboard. "Take one more lesson, Jerry. It won't hurt. We've already paid for it."

I sighed unhappily. "Will you come in with me? Or can you wait out here for me?"

Mum frowned. "Jerry, I've got three errands to make. I'll be back in an hour, I promise."

Reluctantly, I pushed open the car door. "'Bye, Mum."

"If Dr Shreek asks you why you're giving up lessons, just tell him it was interfering with your schoolwork."

"Okay. See you in an hour," I said. I slammed the car door, then watched as she drove away, the tyres crunching over the gravel drive.

I turned and trudged into the school building.

My trainers thudded loudly as I made my way through the dark corridors to Dr Shreek's room.

I looked for Mr Toggle, but didn't see him. Maybe he was in his enormous workshop inventing more amazing things.

The usual roar of piano notes poured from the practice rooms as I passed by them. Through the small, round windows I could see smiling instructors, their hands waving, keeping the beat, their heads swaying to their pupils' playing.

As I turned a corner and headed down another long, dark corridor, a strange thought popped into my head. I suddenly realized that I had never seen another pupil in the corridors.

I had seen instructors through the windows of the rooms. And I had heard the noise of the pupils' playing. But I had never *seen* another pupil.

Not one.

I didn't have long to think about it. A smiling Dr Shreek greeted me outside the door to our practice room. "How are you today, Jerry?"

"Okay," I replied, following him into the room.

He wore baggy grey trousers held up with bright red braces over a crumpled white shirt. His white hair looked as if it hadn't been brushed in a few days. He gestured for me to take my place on the piano bench.

I sat down quickly, folding my hands tensely in my lap. I wanted to get my speech over with quickly before we began the lesson. "Uh . . . Dr Shreek?"

He walked stiffly across the small room until he was standing right in front of me. "Yes, my boy?" he beamed down at me, his Santa Claus cheeks bright pink.

"Well . . . I . . . this will be my last lesson," I choked out. "I've decided I . . . uh . . . have to give up piano lessons."

His smile vanished. He grabbed my wrist. "Oh, no," he said, lowering his voice to a growl. "No. You're not leaving, Jerry."

"Huh?" I cried.

He tightened his grip on my wrist. He was really hurting me.

"Giving up?" he exclaimed. "Not with those hands." His face twisted into an ugly snarl. "You can't give up, Jerry. I need those beautiful hands."

"Let go!" I screamed.

He ignored me and tightened his grip, his eyes narrowing menacingly. "Such excellent hands," he muttered. "Excellent."

"No!"

With a shrill cry, I jerked my wrist free. I leapt up from the piano bench and began running to the door.

"Come back, Jerry!" Dr Shreek called angrily. "You cannot get away!"

He started after me, moving stiffly but steadily, taking long strides.

I pushed open the door and darted out into the corridor. The banging of piano music greeted my ears. The long, dark corridor was empty as always.

"Come back, Jerry!" Dr Shreek called from right behind me.

"No!" I cried out again. I hesitated, trying to decide which way to go, which way led to the

251

front door. Then I lowered my head and started to run.

My trainers thudded over the hard floor. I ran as fast as I could, faster than I'd ever run in my life. The practice rooms whirred past in a dark blur.

But to my surprise, Dr Shreek kept right behind me. "Come back, Jerry," he called, not even sounding out of breath. "Come back. You cannot get away from me."

Glancing back, I saw that he was gaining on me.

I could feel the panic rise in my throat, choking off my air. My legs ached. My heart pounded so hard, it felt as if my chest was about to burst.

I turned a corner and ran down another long corridor.

Where was I? Was I heading towards the front door?

I couldn't tell. This dark corridor looked like all the others.

Maybe Dr Shreek is right. Maybe I *can't* get away, I thought, feeling the blood throb at my temples as I turned another corner.

I searched for Mr Toggle. Perhaps he could save me. But the corridors were empty. Piano music poured out of every room, but no one was out in the corridor.

"Come back, Jerry! There's no use running!"

"Mr Toggle!" I screamed, my voice hoarse and breathless. "Mr Toggle—help me! Help me, please!"

I turned another corner, my trainers sliding on the smoothly polished floor. I was gasping for breath now, my chest heaving.

I saw double doors up ahead. Did they lead to the front?

I couldn't remember.

With a low moan, I stuck out both hands and pushed open the doors.

"No!" I heard Dr Shreek shout behind me. "No, Jerry! Don't go into the recital hall!"

Too late.

I pushed through the doors and bolted inside. Still running, I found myself in an enormous, brightly lit room.

I took a few more steps—then stopped in horror.

The piano music was deafening—like a never-ending roar of thunder.

At first, the room was a blur. Then it slowly began to come into focus.

I saw row after row of black pianos. Beside each piano stood a smiling instructor. The instructors all looked alike. They were all bobbing their heads in time to the music.

The music was being played by—

It was being played by—

I gasped, staring from row to row.

**The music was being played by—*HANDS*!
Human hands floating over the keyboards.
No people attached.
Just *HANDS*!**

My eyes darted down the rows of pianos. A pair of hands floated above each piano.

The instructors were all bald-headed men in grey suits with smiles plastered onto their faces. Their heads bobbed and swayed, their grey eyes opened and closed as the hands played over the keys.

Hands.

Just hands.

As I gaped, paralysed, trying to make sense of what I saw, Dr Shreek burst into the room from behind me. He made a running dive at my legs, trying to tackle me.

Somehow I dodged away from his outstretched hands.

He groaned and hit the floor on his stomach. I watched him slide across the smooth floor, his face red with anger.

Then I spun round, away from the dozens of hands, away from the banging pianos, and started back towards the doors.

But Dr Shreek was faster than I imagined. To my surprise, he was on his feet in a second, moving quickly to block my escape.

I skidded to a stop.

I tried to turn round, to get away from him. But I lost my balance and fell.

The piano music swirled around me. I looked up to see the rows of hands pounding away on their keyboards.

With a frightened gasp, I struggled to my feet.

Too late.

Dr Shreek was closing in on me, a gleeful smile of triumph on his red, round face.

"No!" I cried, and tried to climb to my feet.

But Dr Shreek bent over me, grabbed my left ankle, and held on. "You can't get away, Jerry," he said calmly, not even out of breath.

"Let me go! Let me go!" I tried to twist out of his grip. But he was surprisingly strong. I couldn't free myself.

"Help me! Somebody—help me!" I cried, screaming over the roar of the pianos.

"I need your hands, Jerry," Dr Shreek said. "Such beautiful hands."

"You can't! You *can't!*" I shrieked.

The double doors burst open.

Mr Toggle ran in, his expression confused. His eyes darted quickly around the enormous room.

"Mr Toggle!" I cried happily. "Mr Toggle—help me! He's *crazy!* Help me!"

Mr Toggle's mouth dropped open in surprise. "Don't worry, Jerry!" he called.

"Help me! Hurry!" I screamed.

"Don't worry!" he repeated.

"Jerry, you can't get away!" Dr Shreek cried, holding me down on the floor.

Struggling to free myself, I watched Mr Toggle run to the far wall. He pulled open a grey metal door, revealing some kind of control panel.

"Don't worry!" he called to me.

I saw him pull a switch on the control panel.

Instantly, Dr Shreek's hand loosened.

I pulled my leg free and scrambled to my feet, panting hard.

Dr Shreek slumped into a heap. His hands drooped lifelessly to his sides. His eyes closed. His head sank, his chin lowering to his chest.

He didn't move.

He's some kind of robot, I saw to my amazement.

"Are you okay, Jerry?" Mr Toggle had hurried to my side.

I suddenly realized my entire body was trembling. The piano music roared inside my head. The room began to spin.

I held my hands over my ears, trying to shut out the pounding noise. "Make them stop! Tell them to stop!" I cried.

Mr Toggle jogged back to the control panel and threw another switch.

The music stopped. The hands froze in place

258

over their keyboards. The instructors stopped bobbing their heads.

"Robots. All robots," I murmured, still shaking.

Mr Toggle hurried back, his dark eyes studying me. "Are you okay?"

"Dr Shreek—he's a robot," I uttered in a trembling whisper. If only I could get my knees to stop shaking!

"Yes, he's my best creation," Mr Toggle declared, smiling. He placed a hand on Dr Shreek's still shoulder. "He's really life-like, isn't he?"

"They—they're *all* robots," I whispered, motioning to the instructors, frozen beside their pianos.

Mr Toggle nodded. "Primitive ones," he said, still leaning on Dr Shreek. "They're not as advanced as my buddy Dr Shreek here."

"You—made them all?" I asked.

Mr Toggle nodded, smiling. "Every one of them."

I couldn't stop shaking. I was starting to feel really sick. "Thanks for stopping him. I think Dr Shreek was out of control or something. I—I've got to go now," I said weakly. I started walking towards the double doors, forcing my trembling knees to cooperate.

"Not just yet," Mr Toggle said, placing a gentle hand on my shoulder.

"Huh?" I turned to face him.

"You can't leave just yet," he said, his smile fading. "I need your hands, you see."

"What?"

He pointed to a piano against the wall. A grey-suited instructor stood lifelessly beside it, a smile frozen on his face. There were no hands suspended over the keyboard.

"That will be *your* piano, Jerry," Mr Toggle said.

I started backing towards the double doors one step at a time. "Wh-why?" I stammered. "Why do you need my hands?"

"Human hands are too hard to build, too complicated, too many parts," Mr Toggle replied. He scratched his black, stubbly beard with one hand as he moved towards me.

"But—" I started, taking another step back.

"I can make the hands play beautifully," Mr Toggle explained, his eyes locked on mine. "I've designed computer programmes to make them play more beautifully than any live human can play. But I can't build hands. The pupils must supply the hands."

"But *why*?" I demanded. "Why are you *doing* this?"

"To make beautiful music, naturally," Mr Toggle replied, taking another step closer. "I love beautiful music, Jerry. And music is so much more beautiful, so much more *perfect*, when human mistakes don't get in the way."

He took another step towards me. Then another. "You understand, don't you?" His dark eyes burned into mine.

"No!" I screamed. "No, I *don't* understand! You can't have my hands! You can't!"

I took another step back. My legs were still trembling.

If I can just get through those doors, I thought, maybe I have a chance. Maybe I can outrun him. Maybe I can get out of this crazy building.

It was my only hope.

Gathering my strength, ignoring the pounding of my heart, I turned.

I darted towards the doors.

"Ohh!" I cried out as the ghost woman appeared in front of me.

The woman from my house, from my piano.

She rose up, all in grey except for her eyes. Her eyes glowed red as fire. Her mouth was twisted in an ugly snarl of rage. She floated towards me, blocking my path to the door.

I'm trapped, I realized.

Trapped between Mr Toggle and the ghost.

There's no escape now.

"*I warned you!*" the ghost woman wailed, her red eyes glowing with fury. "*I warned you!*"

"No, please—" I managed to cry in a choked voice. I raised my hands in front of me, trying to shield myself from her. "Please—let me go!"

To my surprise, she floated right past me.

She was glaring at Mr Toggle, I realized.

He staggered back, his face tight with terror.

The ghost woman raised her arms. "*Awaken!*" she wailed. "*Awaken!*"

And as she waved her arms, I saw a fluttering at the pianos. The fluttering became a mist. Wisps of grey cloud rose up from each piano.

I backed away to the doors, my eyes wide with disbelief.

At each piano, the dark mist took shape.

They were ghosts, I realized.

Ghosts of boys, girls, men, and women.

I watched, frozen in horror, as they rose up and claimed their hands. They moved their fingers, testing their hands.

And then, with arms outstretched, their hands fluttering in front of them, the ghosts floated away from their pianos, moving in rows, in single file, towards Mr Toggle.

"No! Get away! Get away!" Mr Toggle shrieked.

He turned and tried to flee through the doors. But I blocked his path.

And the ghosts swarmed all over him.

Their hands pulled him down. Their hands pressed him to the floor.

He kicked and struggled and screamed.

"Let me up! Get off me! Get off!"

But the hands, dozens and dozens of hands, flattened over him, held him down, pushed him face-down on the floor.

The grey ghost woman turned to me. "*I tried to warn you!*" she called over Mr Toggle's frantic screams. "*I tried to scare you away! I lived in your house. I was a victim of this school! I tried to frighten you from becoming a victim, too!*"

"I—I—"

"*Run!*" she ordered. "*Hurry—call for help!*"

But I was frozen in place, too shocked by what I was seeing to move.

As I stared in disbelief, the ghostly hands

swarmed over Mr Toggle and lifted him off the floor. He squirmed and struggled, but he couldn't free himself from their powerful grasp.

They carried him to the door and then out. I followed them to the doorway to watch.

Mr Toggle appeared to be floating, floating into the deep woods beside the school. The hands carried him away. He disappeared into the tangled trees.

I knew he'd never be seen again.

I spun round to thank the ghost woman for trying to warn me.

But she had gone, too.

I was all alone now.

The corridor stretched behind me in eerie silence. Ghostly silence.

The piano music had ended . . . forever.

A few weeks later, my life had pretty much returned to normal.

Dad put an ad in the newspaper and sold the piano straight away to a family on the other side of town. It left a space in the family room, so Mum and Dad got a big-screen TV!

I never saw the ghost woman again. Maybe she moved out with the piano. I don't know.

I made some good friends and was starting to get used to my new school. I was thinking

**seriously of trying out for the baseball team.
I'm not a great hitter, but I'm good in the field.
Everyone says I have great hands.**